Intrigue at a Small Hotel

ELIZABETH COOKE

abbott press

INTRIGUE AT A SMALL HOTEL is a work of fiction. Names, characters, places and incidents are products of the author's imagination or are used fictitiously. Any resemblance to actual events, locales, or persons, living or dead is entirely coincidental.

Abbott Press books may be ordered through booksellers or by contacting:

Abbott Press
1663 Liberty Drive
Bloomington, IN 47403
www.abbottpress.com
Phone: 1 (866) 697-5310

Because of the dynamic nature of the Internet, any web addresses or links contained in this book may have changed since publication and may no longer be valid. The views expressed in this work are solely those of the author and do not necessarily reflect the views of the publisher, and the publisher hereby disclaims any responsibility for them.

Cover design by Todd Engel

ISBN: 978-1-4582-1988-6 (sc)
ISBN: 978-1-4582-1989-3 (hc)
ISBN: 978-1-4582-1990-9 (e)

Library of Congress Control Number: 2016900369

Print information available on the last page.

Abbott Press rev. date: 02/01/2016

PROLOGUE

Intrigue

I APPROACH MY small hotel, Hotel Marcel, on the avenue near The Eiffel Tower in Paris, from a different direction, not on a plane from New York City in the United States, but driving North with Brit in his Peugeot from St. Paul de Vence in the Alpes Maritimes of Southern France.

We have had a delicious sojourn for four days and nights, this first week of October, in that beautiful part of the Côte d'Azur. With the blue Mediterranean across from our bedroom window, in a charming inn outside the town, we have delighted in being together in this place.

While there, I have received enigmatic phone calls from Jean-Luc Marcel, my favorite hotelier in all the world, warning me of a strange, nameless woman who seeks me out. The woman, by her secretive tone of voice, appeared to him to be a menace to me, his friend, Madame Elizabeth. He sounded worried.

And this worries me, as I know Jean-Luc not to be alarmist, not to be overly *dramatique,* and certainly fond enough of me to be concerned about my wellbeing.

As we near the great capital of France, as we gain the *Périphérique,* the main route that rings the city of Paris, I cringe in the bucket seat of Brit's car, in anticipation of what? And I am frightened.

Thank God for Jean-Luc. But thank God, most of all, for Brit, the lover by my side, who gives me the shield of the innocence of a love that with all its vulnerability, provides strength against the unknown.

CHAPTER 1

A Shadow Falls

THE WARNING STARTS this way, at the inn at St. Paul de Vence.

"I have had a strange message. A note – asking about your whereabouts, Elizabeth. Brigitte took the message at the front desk. It was delivered by a messenger service – a boy in uniform."

It is Jean-Luc on the telephone, calling from Hotel Marcel, which I answer at the front desk in the lobby of the delightful inn at St, Paul de Vence, which Brit and I reached only last night. We have just come downstairs, after *café au lait* in our bedroom overlooking the Côte d'Azur.

"What did the note say?"

"It was addressed to me," Jean-Luc says. "The note is brief. It asks do I know where you are? There is left only a telephone number to call. I tried it. It is again a service, a phone service. I inquired who is asking for this personal information. The girl said 'That person's identity is privileged,' to which I replied, "So is Mme. Elizabeth's whereabouts! Privileged! And I hung up."

I sigh. "Thank you, Jean-Luc, I guess." I am perplexed.

"Imagine! How dare whoever this is, try to find out things without revealing the who and the why. It's *dégoutant!*" Jean-Luc is sputtering.

"I agree it's disgusting – but I'm sure it's of no importance. If they send another note or call you…well that would be a different story."

When I hang up, Brit notices my furrowed brow.

"Problem?" he asks.

"No, no. Just a small mystery. Someone wanting to know where I am – not saying who they are or why they want to know."

"That's strange." He takes my hand. "Oh well, beautiful, come on. Let's go for lunch. I want to walk over to *Le Petit Vigneau* – it's a small, local vineyard. I hear they have great wines and a tasting menu. Come on, now. It'll be fun."

"*Bonne idée,*" I reply, and off we set, in jeans and walking shoes, on this fall morning, the sun at its peak and our psyches in step.

It takes less than 20 minutes to make the journey to the vineyard. As we near the *endroit*, in the distance, we see the terraced hills of *Le Petit Vigneau*, the grapes plump and shining on their vines. We spend an hour viewing the property. Then, of greater import, we test the different varietal wines produced in the small shed, with its presses and vats and the verdant, earthy smell of crushed grapes.

Over the third glass, this one, an astonishingly fruity white, the co-owner, Louisa, appears with a tray of *amuses-bouches* –slabs of smoked ham on *croutons*, ewe-milk cheese with bits of *baguette, cornichons*, pungent black olives *Niçoise*.

"A lunch for the Gods!" is Brit's evaluation of this array of delights, to which I can only agree.

This is only our first day on the Côte d'Azur. But as day two, day three, flow effortlessly, Brit has his sketchpad with him at all times. We sit in a field overlooking the blue of the Mediterranean where he is busily absorbed in drawing the vista before him. (I am absorbed too, in watching my love at his work). We walk the hilly, cobbled streets of the little town, visiting the art shops and small *musées* along the way.

The fourth night, we dine on fresh fish, under stars at an outdoor bistro, which provides an upright heater outside against the cooling wind off the water. Later, under a full moon, on the wide terrace of our inn, I watch the barman spear the cork of a bottle of champagne with a saber (one of the 'specialties' at this particular hostelry). As the bubbles fly and leap in the moonlight, I delight in the knowledge that I am on the way to a rendezvous on the second floor of this magic place, in the arms of the man beside me.

Before we rise to go upstairs, the deskman appears on the terrace from inside the lobby with a note addressed to me, a message from Jean-Luc.

His note reads: "Another call - this time a voice, a real person. She says something odd, and I quote, 'Hey, Elizabeth. I'm back. Don't ever under-estimate the power of a woman like me!' The woman's voice was so threatening. She sounded so vindictive. I think you should know about this, Madame. She does not sound like your friend."

She? A woman's voice? 'The power of a woman like me?' Just what woman do I know who is a threat?

And as when the bubbles burst in a glass of champagne, I am left with a very flat taste in my mouth and an acid burn in my throat.

Who? Who in my past? And why?

Most of all, why now?

CHAPTER 2

Le Couvent

IT IS FRIDAY, the 6th of October. Brit is as curious as I concerning the strange woman from my past seeking me out so mysteriously. As we drive north, back to Paris and to the Hotel Marcel, we decide it best I stay there, rather than at Brit's Marais house, in view of the fact someone may be stalking me.

"You will have Jean-Luc to run interference if she comes to the hotel – and of course, policeman René, to put the cuffs on her," Brit says, smiling, trying to relieve my anxiety.

"That's not funny," I respond.

"And of course, I would like to stay upstairs with you too, if that's okay?" he says, his voice tentative.

"More than okay," I say hugging his arm. Even so, the atmosphere in the car is fraught with disturbing internal questions, on my part, and perhaps even suspicions on his.

"Who would want to show up and bug you?" he says, as we turn into a small vegetable stand on the side of the road, to buy some apples, and red ripe tomatoes.

With a *baguette* and some slices of smoked ham from the St. Paul de Vence inn, we make a picnic under a huge aspen tree, on the edge of a grassy field.

"I have no idea," I say, sullenly. And I don't.

"You'd think she'd at least have the balls to identify herself," Brit says, almost angry, biting into an apple with a great crunch.

"Can't we leave the subject of the strange woman? Please," I say, more uncomfortable than I'd like to be.

Returning to the Peugeot, buckling in, I say tentatively, "Could we stop at Sue's on the way?"

"Sure," he says, glancing over at me anxiously.

"She might be able to remember something...someone..."

"I thought you wanted to forget about that mysterious woman."

"I can't."

After a moment, Brit says, "You've known Sue long enough to maybe remember some female person out to trash you?"

"I've known Sue since forever. We were girls together in New York – and at college... and here, in France – when I lived here some years ago. That was before she married her Marquis."

"Wow. A Marquis. How did she manage that?"

"It was a real love story. But that was then. He died a few years ago."

Brit is silent, then, "I never realized you lived in France. When? You never told me."

"Well, no. It didn't seem important."

There is a diffident silence between us. I break it by speaking of Sue. "She might be able to identify just whom I wounded along the way..." my words drift off. Suddenly I feel very, very sleepy.

We pull into Sue's *château, Le Couvent,* late at night. Brit had phoned her earlier from the automobile. My friend was delighted at the thought of our revisit. "Whatever hour of the early dawn you arrive, I'll be waiting," she had responded, her voice aglow as always when she is pleased. "I'll make us omelets."

"No need," Brit had said, laughing. "All we'll need is a bed!"

Tumbling out of the automobile, onto the gravel driveway in front of the *château*, I am surprised to see Sue, in peignoir, standing in the large doorway, with Franco de Peverelli, in dressing robe, at her side. Franco is a recent attachment in Sue's life.

Their welcome is warm and embracing, and Brit and I ascend upstairs quickly to bed. In the morning, we go down to the stone kitchen at the bottom of the building to the aroma of sizzling *pancetta* in a pan, Franco presiding. He is wearing boots and riding breeches, and a clean white shirt. Sue is whisking a bowl of eggs, readying them to scramble in a second pan on the small hot plate.

Over a breakfast, with *café au lait* and warm biscuits accompanying the main event, we speak of the sweetness of St. Paul de Vence, the saber/champagne ritual on the terrace of the inn, and the beauty of the view.

"It's famous," Franco remarks. "Even in Italy...People love 'the sword and the cork ritual'."

As Sue and I take care of the dishes, Franco leads Brit out into the October morning to view the new grape plants he has terraced into the hill to the rear of the *château*.

I tell Sue of Jean-Luc's note from a mysterious person who later phones him with a threat towards me in her voice.

"How weird!" is her first reaction. She pauses in her wiping of a coffee cup. "Now who in the world has it in for you, Elizabeth?"

"I don't know. I am racking my brain. It's a puzzlement."

"Someone from your days in real estate? Someone you did a dirty deal?"

"Oh, come on," I laugh. "That was years ago, and I did not do any dirty deals. Besides, who would be scheming against me over a stupid house or an apartment or an acre of land!"

"Did you steal someone's husband?"

"No."

"Boyfriend?"

"Well, maybe. But nothing so dramatic as to remember years later — and still care about it."

"Hmm," Sue murmurs as she sits down at the breakfast table. "Is there anyone you've harmed in some way, whose money you have made disappear...or whose good name you might have damaged? You know, status is highly important to a certain kind of female."

"Not that I can think of," I say, but all of a sudden, a shadow crosses my mind, a face appears in my memory, and I shake my head. Impossible! How could she hurt me? And why at this moment? I put the whole image out of my mind.

Our two men return, flushed and positive in demeanor.

With more *baguette* and some soft, *Brie* cheese in a little cooler, Brit and I remount our vehicle and continue north on our journey to the City of Light, refreshed. However, as he drives, to the sound of an old Edith Piaf song on the radio, the thoughts in my mind spin uncontrollably around the enigma of a woman who apparently is eager to do me ill.

CHAPTER 3

Fusion Fiasco

ON ARRIVAL AT the Hotel Marcel, Sunday, late afternoon, Brit and I are invited for drinks with Jean-Luc and Isabella at their new apartment across the street in apartment building number 2.

"Any more calls from the mysterious lady?" I ask Jean-Luc. He shakes his head, with the remark, "No, but I am on the case, Madame. Believe me, you will be the first to know."

It is a brief encounter, this evening cocktail, Brit and I being quite exhausted. We decide to have a real 'homecoming' dinner at – of all places – The Maj – as The Majestic Hotel is called, "just to test it again to see if it has improved!" I declare. Jean-Luc calls and makes a reservation. "A Monday dinner experiment", he says with a laugh.

"I think I should ask the Frontenacs," I say. "Perhaps they have news of Duke and Lilith and new little baby?"

And I call, and they accept. I make it clear to one and all that it is my treat.

At 8:00 o'clock Monday evening, October 9th, we assemble in the *Fusion* dining room of the Hotel Majestic, directly next door to Jean-Luc's Hotel Marcel. Our party of six consists of Pierre and Elise Frontenac, Jean-Luc and Isabella, Brit and me.

The black and white décor of the huge entry hall and its bright lighting still manage to affect one with a cold feeling, which we all acknowledge. "I don't know why I insisted on this place," I mutter to Brit.

"An 'experiment' to see if it had changed?" he replies with a grin.

"Bad choice," I say. "Big mistake…ah, well. At least, we are among friends."

"Not all of them," Brit says. "Look over there." And I do, only to see Sylvie LaGrange of the flaming red hair and bold make-up in a low-cut black dress, accompanied by the rake of Paris, Dr. Guillaume Paxière!

"Well, I'll be," I say. They're together again?"

"Guess so," Brit says, as I notice Guillaume looking at me, sending a little wave.

"From your past?" Brit asks.

"You could say so," I say with a little *moue* – "long gone, long forgotten."

Pierre leans forward. "Duke and Lilith are home and happy – she's growing big, he tells me." Pierre has a great smile on his face.

"If it's a girl they're going to name her Eliza – for you, Elizabeth, for me, Elise, and the 'z', especially for his mother, Suzelle." Elise, too, is beaming.

"That's adorable," I say, genuinely pleased.

A waiter in black suit with long white apron approaches with menus. We order drinks and water bottles, and as we peruse the enormous black and white menus, Isabella, leans across Jean-Luc, who is sitting beside me, and whispers, "Why didn't you ask for me?" She is looking at me curiously.

"When?" I am genuinely confused.

"Today. And why aren't you wearing it tonight?"

"What?"

"The new pale green Yves."

"Which?"

"The one with the darker green, cashmere scarf." I look quizzical. "I thought you would surely be sporting it tonight," Isabella continues.

"I have no clue as to what you're talking about." I am mystified.

Isabella looks stunned. "Elizabeth," she starts. "I was upstairs as usual in the atelier. You could have asked for me...."

"I still don't know what you're talking about."

"The dress, silly. The new dress you bought today. At Yves St. Laurent."

"Look, Isabella. I was nowhere near Yves St. Laurent today."

She looks even more nonplussed. "When I went over the receipts earlier this evening, I saw your signature on a credit card slip – it was payment for the green dress."

"What?" Now it is I who am stunned. "Impossible!" I exclaim. "Brit and I were in the Marais all day." The whole tableful of people is silent, listening.

"It's true," Brit says, "at least in the afternoon."

The waiter arrives with our plates of food on a huge tray. Each dish looks more complex and ornate than the next – with sprays of lemon grass, bright red pepper curls, lemon zest and curry paste garnishing the various *entrées*.

As we start to inspect our dinners and attempt to eat, Isabella continues, "I remember thinking what a great purchase you made – the green shift with its darker green scarf. How perfect on you with your dark hair."

"This is ridiculous!" I say, sounding annoyed. Isabella glances at Jean-Luc, who sits there subdued. I see a curious look pass between them.

The dinner party passes in silence as we scrutinize and dissect the food in front of us. After doing as best we can with our various dishes, we all decide to go down the street to the bistro on the corner for coffee and *tartes*. The bistro purchases its desserts from the famed *Le Nôtre*, on an adjacent avenue, and the delicacies are superb. It may assuage our sense of deprivation after this off-putting bizarre *Fusion diner*.

Everyone at the table seems uncomfortable at this moment, but not as uncomfortable as the atmosphere becomes in the next few minutes.

L'Addition for the dinner party arrives on a small silver tray, and I place my credit card upon it. We finish our espressos, the conversation desultory. Many minutes pass, when of a sudden, Nelson, the supercilious manager of The Majestic, and keeper of the desk in the lobby, appears at my side, with the tray and my credit card lying on it.

"Madame," he says, leaning down. "Have you another card?"

"Why?" I ask.

"This has been refused."

"What do you mean?"

"What I say," he half-whispers, hissing, looking down his aquiline nose. "Your card is not accepted."

"No way," I growl. "My account is absolutely up-to-date. The bills are all paid! I made sure before I left the States to come to France." I am outraged, offended.

"Well, I am sorry, Madame," Nelson says, standing straight, reaching his full height. He looks around the table, as Pierre Frontenac gets to his feet and says, *"Pas de problème, Monsieur,"* producing his own card and passing it to Nelson. I notice the expression of disapproval on Elise's face.

Never in all my life have I felt so deflated. As we rise to exit the formidable dining room, I see Sylvie LaGrange and Dr. Guillaume Pàxiere, leaning over their coffee cups and devouring the scene of my humiliation, each with a smirk from ear to ear.

This only compounds my embarrassment, and it is with great effort, I walk past their table with a smile on my face and head held high.

CHAPTER 4

Aha!

"I'VE NEVER BEEN so humiliated in my life!" I down my vodka from the shot glass, straight. "I'm furious!"

"Someone has surely gotten hold of your credit card," Sue says, following suit in the vodka department.

We are sitting on our usual *Caviar Kaspia* banquette, awaiting our lunch. I have been detailing last night's *Fusion* evening to Sue. "First, the green dress. Next, the dinner bill. My card refused!" I pour another vodka shot from its carafe. "That woman. I am not sure it's she, but it has to be."

"I don't know who you're talking about but let's think. Let's eliminate. Do you remember that lawyer you were kind of in love with?"

"You mean Jonathan? Whew. I haven't thought of him lately, although it was pretty intense at the time."

"How long ago…"

"I guess about five years. It was a couple of years after my Bob died. I think I was desperately lonely."

"But could this woman be Jonathan's wife?"

"No, no. In the first place, I don't think she cared – even when we were going at it – She lived in Savannah, Georgia, and he, of course, had the little penthouse in New York. Besides, too much time has passed."

"Probably – but I don't think time has anything to do with a real vendetta. Obviously, this woman hates you. She's trying to ruin your credit, make people distrust you."

"I know and it's driving me crazy. I keep going over and over what I may have done to some woman – to make her so vicious towards me. Oh, Sue, I know I am not a perfect person by any stretch – but I haven't consciously been out to do someone in – not ever."

"Well, darling, you have a somewhat checkered career. Three husbands…"

"Oh, please. I don't count the first. It only lasted months."

"What about David? What about number two spouse?"

"His German call-girl wife…but why? She never recognized I was even alive, and now that he's dead, what would be her point?"

"I hate to bring her up, but what about your daughter… yours and David's - Lisa?"

My lips are closed, my heart too. Then I manage to say, "I haven't spoken with her in 15 years. She told me to go to hell years ago – never knew exactly why…Somewhere, she broke my heart – or maybe I broke hers." At the thought, I begin to feel tears in my eyes.

"Lisa was a complicated kid. She was also kind of bewildered by your divorce from David…split loyalties," Sue says gently. "Besides, it's a kind of truth, that although she was sweet looking and very dear, to have a beautiful, dynamic mother, can be hard for a young girl to take. It's kind of a classic scenario."

"Are you saying I was beautiful? That's ridiculous. I was just another pretty girl."

"No way, baby. You were beautiful partly because you have a luminous quality." Sue pats my hand. "You still have that, you know."

"Now you're being kind."

Sue shakes her head. "It just beams out of you. You can't help it," she says with a smile.

Our baked potatoes, fluffed high with butter and sour cream and topped with caviar, arrive. This is my absolutely favorite dish in all the world, baked potatoes with butter and sour cream being the ultimate soul food, and caviar the sexiest manna from heaven.

As I start, after the first bite, I find my eyes filling with tears. I lay down my fork, take a sip of vodka from the tiny shot glass. A thought that kills my enjoyment of my favorite dish must be dire. "Oh, Sue. Who? What? Why?"

"Well, if it's not thwarted love, then it's money driving her – or the lack of it."

"But I've never stolen…"

"Stolen? Of course not – but deprived someone? Hurt their earning power? Ruined their reputation?"

That's it! Reputation! Status!

And suddenly I know. I know exactly who this vindictive SHE must be.

CHAPTER 5

Bonny Brandeis

BONNY BRANDEIS.

Bonny is not a true Brandeis. She had been briefly married to a great grandson of Louis Brandeis, the first Jewish Supreme Court Justice. Born Benita Bow, in a small town in southern Georgia, she decides to keep the prestigious name, Brandeis, as an entrée into New York City society.

It works, initially. Good looking, with bright blonde hair and green eyes, Bonny, as she is called, hits the big apple at the early age of 23. She had been to community college in Macon, where she majored in art history, and won a beauty contest, "Miss Southern Georgia," a title of which she is inordinately proud. She is also bright, in a sharp way, always looking for the opportunity – or the man – who can advance her position and feather her nest. She is seductive, but also the ultimate narcissist, and finally, something of a thief.

After her Brandeis divorce, she lives with a Wall Street mini-tycoon, (part time because he is married). About eight years ago, she manages, through her 'friend's' large donations to a well-known New York Charity that benefits children with chronic diseases, named "A Child's Voice," to become a member of its board of directors. After a year or two, with extra donations from her benefactor, (and, in all fairness, because she makes good suggestions), Bonny is elected President of the board. My, she's proud.

I am some years older than the new president and have been on the board of "A Child's Voice' as acting secretary for 15 years. When Bonny Brandeis, always in designer clothes, presides over the monthly meetings, I am continually surprised by her extreme interest in Wall Street trading. Bonny, singlehandedly, places a young man from a firm in that prestigious area of New York City on the board as treasurer. It is important, of course, for the charity's portfolio, to invest as advantageously as possible, but I am acutely aware of how avidly Bonny takes notes on the young man's every word.

"A Child's Voice" is in the practice of giving huge, yearly galas to raise money for the hospitals connected to the charity. They take place at the Plaza Hotel, or in the grand ballroom of The Pierre Hotel. An auction is always held, whereby the wealthy attendees can bid for items on display – art works (donated by connoisseurs), trips to Paris (donated by chic Paris hotels), expensive dinner parties (donated by restaurants like The Twenty One Club and Daniel Boulud), even large gift cards to couturiers, like Carolina Herrera and Ralph Lauren. It's all in the game.

Suddenly, the past leaps up to face me. All is intensely vivid.

Six years ago, the gala is held in the Plaza Hotel Grand ballroom. Bonny Brandeis is extremely visible that night, in a crimson evening dress, as the charity's new president. At the following board meeting a few days later, the event is analyzed and the amount of money raised assessed. I am asked to take the minutes. This is a new demand for me. There is always a secretary from the office to actually take down the words of the meeting. As acting secretary, my usual chores involve signing documents, and managing certain letter-writing campaigns for donations. It has never been to actually transcribe the minutes.

This day, however, the usual charity secretary is ill, so it's incumbent upon me to take the minutes.

"I hate taking minutes. I'm not good at it," I protest. "I'm too detailed." I remember the copious notes I took at lectures while at Vassar College.

"Sorry, but there's no one else," Bonny insists so I do as expected and take down every word. And I mean word for word. The result is devastating.

To whom?

To Bonny.

At the next meeting the following month, when the minutes are read, it turns out that Bonny has revealed she has taken a trip to Paris staying for a week at the Plaza Athénée, all expenses paid by that hotel. She never accepted any bid for it at the auction at the Gala. The minutes designate that Bonny has used two of the courturier gift cards to put clothes on her back, never accepting any bid from the attendees at the gala; that she held a large dinner party at The Twenty-One Club, all expenses paid, and that items donated from Macy's Department store (elegant china, silverware, table linens) now grace her small apartment in Tudor City (the rent paid for by her Wall Street companion).

That year's gala for the benefit of "A Child's Voice" brought in only $80,000, when usually the proceeds exceed more than $250,000. The entire board is not only disappointed but deeply disturbed.

When my minutes are reviewed by the board members, (16 persons in all), there is general consternation and frankly, a mask of fury on the face of Bonny Brandeis.

I have brought her down and her look of pure hatred toward me is chilling.

Didn't she realize she brought it on herself? After all, it was she who insisted on my taking the minutes, even as I was hesitant. More important, it was she and she alone who committed the offenses in question, not anyone else.

Somehow, someone (not me) leaks the story to The New York Daily News, and the New York Post, who write rather vicious – but true – articles about the "venal president of a children's charity who lines her own purse, deflecting funds dedicated to caring for children with lethal diseases."

Both papers nickname Bonny Brandeis, "The Greedy Philanthropist" and there is a picture of her, in ball gown, in each paper. She is even ridiculed with this name on "The Late Show" and accused of 'hating children who are ill.'

Of course, Bonny immediately is forced to leave the board in disgrace, (shortly after which I find I am elected president).

Life goes on. It is six years later. I resigned from "A Child's Voice" after more than 20 years of service, just last year. Enough is enough, I had decided. I would always contribute money, but the time had come to move on to other pursuits. And Bonny was long since out of sight, out of mind.

Until now. Until Paris. Until the Hotel Marcel.

It has to be she! I have racked my brains, and Bonny Brandeis is the only logical culprit, a woman rather vicious by nature, and vengeful of character, who is more than capable of carrying a grudge.

I have no doubt in my mind that Bonny Brandeis is my nemesis.

CHAPTER 6

A Cabal

"AT LEAST WE know who she is and more important, where!" Sue announces, as we – Jean-Luc, Isabella, Franco, Brit and myself –huddle over a corner table at *Le Bosquet,* at the rear of the 2nd tier of the restaurant.

"Yeah," Brit chimes in. "I couldn't believe it. There's this blonde woman in a green dress at my front door. She's standing in the rain with a huge umbrella over her head with the logo 'The Maj' in bright red."

"She had a nerve," I mumble, upset at the whole idea Bonny has discovered Brit's house in the Marais district.

"She gave her name – Bonny Brandeis – and told me she would like to see some paintings," Brit goes on. "She has heard of my work. I told her I used a gallery but she insisted. 'As long as I'm here…you can't keep a lady waiting in the rain, now can you?'"

The thought of her flirtatious coyness with my Brit made me blanche.

In the center of the table are two plates of warm *Camembert* cheese, in which we dip crusts of *baguette.* There are two bottles of *Cabernet*

Sauvignon, one at each end of the table, a third waiting on a shelf next to our table.

"It would be The Majestic! *naturellement,*" says Jean-Luc cynically.

"Do you think she realizes I know she's there?" I ask.

"Probably," Brit says. "After all, she did come to my house, and she may know I'm…" and he looks at me. "With you – that we're… It's just by chance I saw 'The Maj' on the umbrella she was carrying. 'Course it was hard to miss."

"It's more than likely that she knows you are at *chez* Hotel Marcel," Jean-Luc declares, turning to me. "Willie claims she is preening around The Majestic like she owns it, but I don't think she thinks YOU realize that SHE'S right next door."

"And Willie would know!" I exclaim. Willie Blakely, formerly worked in the Majestic dining room. He is now manager for Jean-Luc at Hotel Marcel, having left the massive hotel next door in disgust.

"Sure Willie would know. He still has friends at the hotel – old waiter friends – and I think a particular young Asian chambermaid," Jean-Luc answers me. "Her name is Ana Wi – and he is quite taken."

I have to smile. "Good for Willie."

"As for what's her name – Bonny Brandeis? Is that it?" Jean-Luc continues. "I'm sure she avoids running into you at all costs, at least for the moment. René seems to think she has spies out to monitor your comings and goings."

"It's inevitable you two will see each other sooner or later," Isabella comments.

"I am so angry at her," Sue says, frowning, "really furious. She's tried to ruin you. Now I want to ruin HER." She digs deep with a piece of *baguette* into the runny cheese, pops the morsel into her mouth.

"You know," she continues, "I have an idea."

"We could use one," Brit mutters.

"What if I seek her out? She doesn't know who I am or that you and I are big buds," Sue says turning to me. "Supposing I 'befriend her,' butter-her-up, - even invite her out to *Le Couvent…*"

"What?" Franco is appalled. "Why would you want a crooked lady like that one in your home?"

"Oh, Franco. It would just be to give her a false sense of importance… kind of pull her fangs…make it even a farther fall when we finally pull her down!"

Brit laughs. "Wow, Sue! You're scaring me."

Sue looks at Franco. " You're probably right, *mon ami*. Why poison my home! But I mean it. I'm outraged! Look what she's done to my friend. I intend to blow her sky high." And Sue casts such a woeful look in my direction that we all start to giggle.

"The higher she gets, the harder the fall, right?" Sue goes on.

"The more inflated, the bigger the bust!" Franco exclaims in his Italian-accented French, which brings a burst of laughter from our little conspiracy

As the humor dies down, Sue says, "Look. Seriously, I may even have to bad mouth my friend here to gain Bonny's confidence, find out how she accomplished all this."

"Uh oh," Brit says, glancing at me.

"No problem," I say overly bright. "Say all the terrible things you want – that I'm selfish, eager to hurt anyone who gets in my way, that I deliberately set out to be cruel…say anything that will get her to say how she managed to…exploit…"

"You mean, how she managed to screw you…" Brit is angry. Turning to Sue, he says, " just find out all her nasty little manipulations, all the dirty little tricks up her sleeve. Then, we'll go to René."

"*Eh bien*," Jean-Luc breaks in. "It's a plan."

"Yes," I respond with a sigh. "At least we have a plan."

Sue is tapping the table with a forefinger as we finish the main course of *canard confit* and a *sauté* of potatoes. "I have to figure out how to make the connection. How will I know her?"

"You'll know her alright," I say, "a blatant blonde American. She has green eyes…"

"And a small figure," says Isabella. "I know that much because I saw the dress receipt for the green dress."

"Well, I'm not going to sit around the lobby of The Majestic, waiting to see a small blonde in a green dress walk by. Ah, well," she says, still tapping. "I'll think of something."

And knowing Sue, she will! I smile at her and say, "At least we have a plan."

"That we have, dear heart. That we have!" is her reply.

CHAPTER 7

A Special Déjeuner

SUE CONTRIVES A way to meet Bonny Brandeis. She goes to The Majestic Hotel and after presenting her Marquise credentials, inquires of Nelson, the manager, if there happen to be any American women at the hotel, that she is forming a committee of her compatriots to produce an article about their feelings for Paris and France itself.

"It is for the spring issue of French *Vogue*," she tells Nelson in her most high-handed manner.

And Nelson is impressed.

Thus, Sue has been able to approach Bonny Brandeis. She has done it skillfully, using her title of Marquise and the name of the prestigious magazine, *Vogue*, to whet the woman's appetite for status. She invites Bonny Brandeis to lunch.

My dear friend has chosen – not our beloved *Caviar Kaspia* –'I wouldn't desecrate the place with that woman's presence,' she tells me, but a lovely restaurant on the Right bank not far from the Louvre.

Sue puts on her most Marquise-like persona. Believe me, she knows exactly how to do it. And poor old Bonny Brandeis is grist for Sue's mill.

"First, I order martinis for the two of us," Sue says on the phone. "I had learned that a martini was catnip to Bonny. Willie tells me he heard she apparently orders them - more than one – repeatedly at The Majestic bar." Sue is describing to me the scene at *La Rose Blanche* during her luncheon with Bonny Brandeis yesterday.

"'How lovely,' the brassy blonde woman says and the martini is gone in minutes. By the way, she is wearing that green dress – no scarf – but it is quite stunning – although SHE is not."

"Tell me more." I am salivating with curiosity.

"Well! I learned a bunch. You wouldn't believe how much she told me, over the second drink, and by the third, she was positively delighting in revealing every nasty little ploy."

"Do go on. I can't wait to hear."

"First she tells me about being on the board of 'A Child's Voice,' a charity she has come to despise. I ask her, 'Why? Doesn't it benefit sick children?' and she says yes, but she had a bad experience with one of the board members, a horrible woman who wanted her job. 'I was president, you know,' and she announces this so proudly, I want to throw up. Anyway, then she expounds on this woman – you – who were so jealous that you connived with the rest of the board to frame her and get rid of her. 'That awful bitch then became president! Can you believe it?' Oh, Bonny went on and on."

I begin to laugh, although underneath I am so angry I can hardly speak. "What next?" I ask.

"Well," Sue begins, "she continued about how she is going to have 'retribution,' that this woman will 'pay,' that she knows exactly how and where to ruin her good name. This is after ordering her third martini!"

"You got her drunk?"

"I didn't get her drunk. She did that all by herself. I just sat there, barely sipping my first one, and the two of us each toying with a *Coquille St. Jacques*, for which the restaurant happens to be renowned."

"Did she mention my name?"

"I asked her who the woman that had been so awful to her was – and she did tell me, but she cautioned me to secrecy because, as she said, 'that woman is in Paris at this very moment!'"

"Oh, lord," I sigh. "How did she know that?"

"I have yet to find that out. But, nothing daunted, I said, 'you, know, Bonny, I think I have met this woman' – you, of course – and she practically fell off her chair, although she was already pretty sloppy and might have fallen off it anyway." Sue is laughing.

I laugh too at the picture of Bonny in her green dress, her green eyes bloodshot, and barely upright at the luncheon table.

"She really is getting sloppy, at this point, and it's close to three o'clock in the afternoon, so I tell her I have to drive back to Montoire to my *château*..."

"'You live in a *château*?' she cries out so loudly that people turned to look – and it was then that I invited her to come down to spend the night."

"You didn't!"

"I did too. You want me to get this right, no? Well, there's a lot more I have to find out. How she is doing this...this...identity theft – this trashing of your credit – and more important, does she have an accomplice. I really think she is too dumb to have contrived all this on her own. And, baby doll, I intend to find out who!"

"God bless you, Sue," I blurt out, and I mean it from the bottom of my heart.

CHAPTER 8

Super Shock

ON DECENDING TO go to dinner late on Friday, Brit and I are met at the desk by Jean-Luc. In his hand is a Western Union telegram addressed to me.

"I have not seen one of those in forever," Brit exclaims, as I tear the envelope open.

On the page is my name, the address of the Hotel Marcel and the following words:

> *Congratulations on the down payment for*
> *the hotel particulier, located at 13 rue Monsieur,*
> *75007, Paris France. We have received from the Chase*
> *Bank, 72nd Street in New York City, the amount of*
> *$75,000 (or approx.55,000 euros) from your Savings*
> *account # 8664345.*

Please contact: Toinette Minet, Realtor
23 Bis, rue de Charlot,
75007, Paris
Tel: 01 45 26 31 92
And again. Congratulations on acquiring such a fine property.

I feel ready to faint, as Brit leads me to a chair in the salon, Jean-Luc grabs a pot of black coffee and a brandy bottle and pours both in a cup, half and half.

CHAPTER 9.

Montoire Desecrated

ON THE MONDAY, after Sue's lunch at *La Rose Blanche*, and Bonny's overnight visit to *Le Couvent* on the weekend, Sue decides to come into Paris specifically to report to me and to Brit, her latest findings. And they are *formidable!*

Sue arrives with Franco at her side at the Hotel Marcel, and the four of us walk across to Jean-Luc's apartment on the 5th floor of apartment #2 in the late afternoon. Isabella, of course, joins us there after her work at Yves St. Laurent is completed for the day. Also, at this *petite soirée*, is a special guest, the detective/policeman René Poignal.

"I thought he should be here," Jean-Paul announces, "because there is mischief afoot and undoubted legal offenses."

Frankly, I am deeply relieved René is with us.

After filling wine glasses and presenting warm pecan nuts in a bowl, and a platter with a variety of cheese and crisp crackers, we all sit about the room awaiting what?

"Tell us, Madame La Marquise," Jean-Luc starts. "What have you discovered?"

"Amazing things," Sue says with a smile. "All I can say is, what a small world." She looks spectacular in a navy suit and white chiffon blouse. "Our little Miss Bonny has been a busy lady – and not alone in the conspiracy to destroy my friend here, my dear Elizabeth."

"Tell us, for God sakes, Sue," I cannot help but blurt out. "It's my fate on the line here." I am still in shock over the Western Union telegram that wiped out my savings. I have yet to call the realtor, Toinette Minet. Jean-Luc wants his lawyer involved before I speak with her. In fact, he has arranged an appointment for me with Jacques Ballon, Esq. for Wednesday morning. I did call the Chase Bank in New York to try to block the money transfer. Too late! I am really up the creek and feel as though I am dead broke.

"I must say Bonny Brandeis is a very chatty person," Franco says. "I really didn't want her to come to the *château* – but it is well she did, because she just couldn't stop talking."

"And Franco kept pouring the wine!" Sue says with a smile. "Her glass was never empty."

"Just how did this person acquire Madame Elizabeth's personal information?" René asks. "It is high theft, after all."

"I can just repeat what she told us," Sue says. "She had the sense to take documents, when she left the charity – documents with information about Elizabeth on them – her credit card number – even with the three numbers on the back of the card and the expiration date. One charitable donation folder even had Elizabeth's Savings Bank account number – Chase Bank on 72nd Street – it was in there – visible – because, at the time, my friend here made an extra large contribution to 'A Child's Voice.' But worst of all, her Social Security number was all over the place."

"I deleted all those numbers when I resigned," I say weakly.

"Yes, but too late," says Sue. "Bonny left several years before that time, while you were still presiding."

"Unbelievable," Brit explodes, standing and walking about the room.

"Bonny went on about how careless, Elizabeth was, leaving all that personal information around for all the world to see. Careless? 'Oh no, more like stupid!' she exclaimed. I could have swatted her."

"I kept pouring her more of the *Sauvignon Blanc*," Franco says proudly.

"So why have you waited so long to use this information, Bonny dear?" Sue is mimicking herself.

"'It had to be just right. And then, I got lucky,' Bonny said smugly, taking a big swig of wine. 'Only just recently. I'd waited almost six years to get back at Elizabeth, but then, opportunity struck.'"

"'Opportunity?' I asked." Sue is well into the story.

"'More like a man!' Bonny said. Oh she was so smug! 'It's always a man. Seems to be my *forté!*' When she said that, I thought I was going to throw up." Sue is shaking her head.

"Then, curling up on my damask couch, real conspiratorial, Bonny said, 'a couple of weeks ago, I get back to New York from Florida, and by sheer chance,' funny she had forgotten about Elizabeth for a moment – anyway, she goes to this big do at the Plaza Hotel. 'The guy I'm with' Mr. Nameless,' Bonny went on – 'he's big in PR – and was promoting this charity event for cancer.'"

By this time, René is crouched next to Sue, absorbed in the narrative.

"I couldn't help but remark that she of all people would know about charity events, after her experience with 'A Childs Voice,'" Sue continues. "Bonny is well into the wine by now. She ignores my comment and says, 'Whose table is directly next to the one where we're sitting? Of all people, one of the sheiks that owns the Plaza! And in fact, he has a suite there – I believe a whole floor.'"

"I suddenly turned cold," Sue says. "It can't be. *Quelle coïncidence!* 'A sheikh?' I ask her. 'Does he have a name?'"

"'Of course,' Bonny responds, quite nasty. 'His name is Hamad al-Boudi.' I think I'm going to pass out."

"I think I may pass out too," I exclaim, as a collective 'no!' is emitted from our little group.

"This has got to be her accomplice," continues Sue. "'Did you actually meet him?' I ask her."

"'Naturally,' she says. 'After all the food and several drinks – you know, I thought Arabs didn't drink – but this Hamad – he manages to down quite a few – and, well, he had been eyeing me and suddenly he gets up – full robes and all - and asks me to dance.'" "'He did?' I said. 'Pretty rare thing to do for an Arabic man.'"

"'Yeah, but he was smitten for the moment,' Bonnie says, all puffed up and preening."

"'Where was Mr. Nameless?' I asked her."

"'Oh, I couldn't care less about him,' she says. 'Hamad and me – off we go to the adjoining bar. He tells me it's my blonde hair that got him. Anyway, we talk. He gets kind of maudlin…starts telling me about a daughter who went wild in Paris – threw off her burka – and all because of this nosey American woman who encouraged her to whore around Paris and go off and marry some black guy. When he mentioned her name, I nearly dropped my teeth. Elizabeth! By God, Elizabeth!' Believe me, I was in shock too," Sue exclaims.

"'And Hamad knew exactly where Elizabeth would be,' Bonny went on, 'because she loves that lowly little Hotel Marcel. That's how I came to find her,' Bonny continued, puffing away on her cigarette. 'Hamad al-Boudi. How about that.'"

How about that!

CHAPTER 10

Reflections

I AWAKE TUESDAY morning, mind and conscience blurred with the details Sue has presented yesterday about Bonny Brandeis and her co-conspirator Hamad al-Boudi. The hate-filled sheikh is a mirror image of the hate-filled woman. They make a menacing pair.

Brit is not with me this morning, and I feel lonely without him, bemused and fearful, which leads to a kind of self-disgust.

"Enough self-pity," I say out loud, and rouse myself up to dress for the day ahead.

I realize that it has been more than a week since Brit and I returned to Paris from St. Paul de Vence, extending my sojourn in France to over three full weeks. I had planned on two and have pressing issues to deal with at home; my son and his family and his new business venture, closing of the house in Long Island, charitable events I have committed to - (none of which are 'A Child's Voice'). But I realize that there is no way to return to the States until some of my credit problems are dealt with, and the issue of Bonny Brandeis is resolved.

I'm stuck in Paris!

I'm stuck at the Hotel Marcel. I'm stuck with Brit and Jean-Luc and Isabella and René and Giscard and Sasha and Ray and Sue and Franco, and oh my goodness, what a way to be stuck!

I decide I will go out and about and enjoy this lovely city, its every sensory temptation, its every visual delight, and putting on my best suit and Dries van Noten coat, I step forward into a crisp and glistening mid-November day in Paris.

The air is invigorating. The sky is blue. I walk down to the Seine, past Les Invalides, and across the bridge, arriving on the Right Bank and the hill up the avenue Montaigne toward the Étoile.

I do not let negative thoughts deter my mood, even as I reflect on a conversation I happened to overhear between Jean-Luc and Elise Frontenac. It was the day after our *Fusion* evening, the night of humiliation over the rejection of my credit card. That *débâcle*, I knew, had not gone unregistered by Elise Frontenac.

It was in the lobby of Hotel Marcel. Elise had come over to see Jean-Luc, who happened to be manning the front desk. It was about noon. Her pretense was to bring him a house-warming gift for his new apartment across the street. "I meant to give it to you and Isabella days ago – but you know how things can get busy," she had told him with a coy little laugh. "It's just an orchid plant but I thought it would look so pretty in the room Isabella just decorated."

Of course, they had no idea I was in the back of the salon over a *café au lait*.

Jean-Luc was effusive in his reaction. "Ah, Madame – how very kind of you." This conversation was in French, but I was sufficiently fluent to understand every word, every nuance, as I heard her say, "You know, I was so surprised last night with…you know…"

"I know what?" Jean-Luc said.

"You know. With the business of the check."

"The check?" Thank God he was playing dumb.

"The credit card. Elizabeth's credit card...She is such a likeable woman, but my goodness. I hope, Jean-Luc she is able to pay her bills here at the hotel..."

"Of course she does," he says gruffly. Then, "Ah, yes. I remember now...the credit card ...a minor incident. By the way, she left money here at the desk to repay your husband..." I hear him open a drawer. "Let's see, how much was it?"

"Oh, oh," she says. "I did not come to the hotel for that." She sounds quite disconcerted.

"I'm sure you didn't," he says firmly, as I hear him counting out euro bills. "Is this sufficient?"

"Oh, my. I think that's too much."

"No, no. I am sure Elizabeth would want it this way – for the trouble and inconvenience. And now, Madame, I am afraid I have to get back to work...my accounting..." and I hear him sit down at the desk.

"Yes. Yes. And thank you, Jean-Luc. Thank you very much," and I hear her tentative steps out the door.

When I am sure she has gone, I creep around the corner of the salon and go up to Jean-Luc at the front desk.

He looks up? "You heard?" at which I nod. "C'est une femme absurde!"

"No, no. I can hardly blame her. But you, Jean-Luc. You are un homme magnifique! I thank you," and I lean across and grab his hand. "I owe you sir, and you absolutely know I'll pay you back."

He leans back in his chair. "How long have I known you, Madame Elizabeth?"

"Like forever," I say with a grin.

"Exactly! Now run along. I really do have work to do."

The memory of his kindness brings a bounce to my step, as I leave the Hotel Marcel this Tuesday morning. I find myself on the avenue Montaigne, my step still bouncing all the way up the hill and into a tiny bistro where I order their most delicious *soupe à l'oignon* and a large glass of *Cabernet Sauvignon*. Now who could ask for anything more! Such an elegant repast, and such a friend like Jean-Luc Marcel!

CHAPTER 11

Jacques Ballon, Esq.

MY WEDNESDAY MEETING with the lawyer, Monsieur Jacques Ballon at 11:00 AM is not truly satisfactory, although I do feel more secure to have a legal person in my corner. A portly fellow, behind an old fashioned desk in an art deco building on the Right Bank, Jacques (he insists I call him that), is deferential and kind. Jean-Luc accompanies me, which is deeply appreciated.

I do not ask Brit to join this expedition. It is not his cup of tea, first of all, and frankly, I feel guilty about keeping him from his works of art. He is at his house in the Marais, painting his heart out.

Before addressing the Toinette Minet, Realtor, issue, and my unacknowledged 'purchase' of a house, from Jacques' desk, I call my old friend (and ex lover) Jonathan Markham at his office in Manhattan. We have kept in touch over the years, friendly and dispassionate.

I explain to him my predicament, that Bonny Brandeis, of all people, is back in my life, determined to up-end it; the green dress, my credit card rejection, worst of all, 13 rue Monsieur. I try to tell him of Hamad al-Boudi's involvement in the whole scheme. This is hard because, although Jonathan well knew Bonny, as he was long on the board of 'A Child's Voice,' and present for Bonny's unseemly dismissal, a sheikh from Qatar is a different story. Hamad al-Boudi is an elaborate embellishment that is difficult indeed for Jonathan to wrap his head around. I can hardly blame him.

"Qatar? Really Elizabeth. How in the world...?"

"Don't ask," I respond. "Look," I continue, after explaining how Bonny had access to my sensitive numbers and information, stolen from our charity documents, "I have to protect whatever funds are left in my account. I called the Chase Bank and the $75,000 has already been transferred to this realtor to buy a house in the 7th Arrondissement here in Paris..."

"Of course, this is fraud of the worst kind," Jonathan iterates, sputtering. "What a woman, that Brandeis dame! It's so damn blatant."

"Can you help me, Jonathan? I really am in trouble."

"Of course, old friend. I'll do what I can."

After giving him my phone number at Hotel Marcel, (as well as the pertinent business numbers in question), I turn back to Jacques and the issue of Toinette Minet. Just how do we approach her and hopefully, get back my $75,000.

"Very carefully," is his first response. "I want to be extremely cautious with this lady," Jacques says in his heavily French-accented English. "We do not want to...inform..."

"Tip her off?" Jean-Luc suggests.

"Ah, yes...tip her off, Madame Bonny Brandeis. The less she knows we are aware of her plots, the better. We must be discreet!" Jacques begins to relish the whole inexplicable riddle. "But first – you have called the credit card company?"

"Yes. My card had been cancelled only a couple of day ago – supposedly by me. Of course, it was Bonny, pretending to be me – and it was after she bought the dress at Yves St. Laurent with it."

"Is it possible to get the receipt for the dress purchase from Yves St. Laurent?" Jacques asks.

"Absolutely," Jean-Luc chimes in. "My wife works at Yves' atelier. She can surely obtain it. She is quite *éminent* in that establishment," he adds proudly.

"I tried to order a new master card," I continue, "but they insisted that I had already ordered one – that very day - that they were overnighting it to the Hotel Majestic, c/o the manager. 'Why the manager?' I asked. Their answer was that 'I' had told them, because of the theft of my original card, 'I' was mistrustful and very cautious. Can you imagine?" I am shaking my head, as is the lawyer, Jacques Ballon.

"So Bonny has – or will soon have – the ability to charge new purchases in your name on this new card." Jacques looks quizzical and extremely serious.

"Exactly! My God," I say. "How can I stop her?"

"Someone will have to get hold of that card. Is there anybody close to her?" Jacques inquires.

"No," says Jean-Luc. "But you're right. We have to get hold of that credit card."

"Naturally I will have no money to pay for anything, anyway! None of this makes sense," I say with a bitter laugh, because the whole business seems so ludicrous.

Jean-Luc and I leave the good barrister's office rather downhearted, yet determined to extricate me from the mess I am in.

"I will be sure to retrieve that receipt," he assures me as we find a cab at a taxi stand on the avenue Kleber. "I think we should get René involved, don't you?"

"The sooner, the better," I exclaim. "René may be the answer…"

"I wouldn't expect too much of him," Jean-Luc says, patting my hand. "But surely he will be able to advise us on further moves. He is a good detective and quick to move. Besides, he likes you, and I am sure he will want to – how you say – 'save your bacon'?"

"Oh, Jean-Luc," I say, bursting out laughing. I had been ready to cry, but 'save my bacon' dried up any tear that might have fallen. "Jean-Luc, you are too much," and I lean over and kiss him on the cheek.

CHAPTER 12

Giscard Poignal

ON THURSDAY, AROUND noon, I am waiting in the hallway by Jean-Luc's office, for the *ascenseur* to go upstairs, my packages, from a trip to the Monoprix store, in hand. From the stairway abutting the elevator, a figure emerges. The man looks like a New York gangster from a film *noir*, black suit, black shirt, long black tie, and a cut-down cowboy hat tilted over a raised eyebrow.

He is quite startling in appearance, the serious face handsome, with thin lips and a cleft in his chin. He lifts his hand to the brim of his hat in salute, as he passes me.

At this moment, Jean-Luc's office door swings open and the hotelier appears, with a big smile, and a loud, "Giscard!" and then, "Madame Elizabeth. You meet in the hall? Please come in," and he waves the two of us through the doorway and into his office.

I sit on the chair opposite Jean-Luc's desk, which he stands behind. The man named Giscard remains in the doorway.

"Elizabeth, this is Giscard Poignal, René's younger brother."

"How do you do," Giscard says removing the brimmed hat, revealing a head of thick, dark hair. He really is handsome, so different from his brother's demeanor. René is so much more conventional looking, a bit plump, with a nervous, wary look. Then, after all, he is a policeman and has the right to look wary.

"Giscard is here from Barcelona, arrived last night. How long do you plan to stay in Paris?" Jean-Luc asks.

"Don't know," Giscard responds. "Depends."

"On what?"

Giscard smiles. "On any number of things," he says. "But largely, money."

"Doesn't surprise me," Jean-Luc says wryly. "In fact," he says with a frown, "I would expect no less." I am astonished that this rather unsavory bit of information is iterated before a stranger. Me.

"What is your business in Barcelona," I say to quickly change the atmosphere. "Such a beautiful city."

"Yes, it is beautiful," Giscard says, visibly relieved at the change in conversation. "I am a welder." I notice his English is quite perfect, only slightly tinged with a Latin cast.

"A welder?" I say. "I don't think I've ever met a welder before. What do you weld?"

"Valves, pipe fittings, for large industrial construction – I am here for the International Exposition at the Grand Palais – actually architectural and sculptural pieces that use the anvil, which of course is what I use in my shop - but of course, my work is strictly practical…not so artistic."

"I think of an anvil as, I don't know…horse shoes," I say, laughing.

"Well, you are quite right," Giscard says amiably. "In fact, I use an anvil all the time. But not for horse shoes," again shooting me his great smile.

"You speak perfect English," I say. Jean-Luc looks kind of sour, sitting at his desk. He senses the flirtatious atmosphere in the room between Giscard and myself, not that I am interested that way – Brit has devoured any such temptation – but this man surely knows women, loves women, and probably uses them unmercifully.

"I lived in Atlanta, Georgia, for almost 18 years," he says.

"Really! What did you do there?"

"I welded," he says with a laugh.

I bet he welded many a woman in the course of his *travail*.

At this moment, René arrives.

I am struck by how different the two men are, as they embrace, René patting Giscard's back in greeting. There is a warmth between them, but I sense, too, a kind of distance. It is as if René is the disapproving father, rather than brother. He seems much older than Giscard, fiftyish, graying, whereas Giscard has the vigorous stance of youth, although I learn from Jean-Luc later, that there is only a three-year difference in age.

The two are speaking in rapid French. They smile, gesticulate, ask questions, one of the other, when René turns to me and says, "Ah, Madame Elizabeth. I see you have met *mon frère*. I must warn you. He has a special way with the ladies."

"I'm sure he does," I say, a little surprised at this remark. "Forewarned is forearmed," I continue, at which René gives a wise little smile, nods to Jean-Luc and says to him, "*Merci, mon ami, pour l'accomodation.*"

"*Pas de problème.* Your brother is always welcome at my hotel. You are off?" Jean-Luc asks, as the two brothers turn to the office door. "You go to the Grand Palais?"

"Yes," René says. "To the Expo – and then a fat lunch where we can catch up," and he touches Giscard's back. "*Allons-y?*" and the two leave, René leading the way.

I sit there for a moment. "Giscard is staying here?"

"*Oui*," Jean-Luc says. "For nothing…no room fee. I do it for René. He doesn't want his brother *chez lui*."

"What an interesting fellow," I can't help but remark.

"That he is. That he is, *bien sûr*," replies Jean-Luc, busily shifting papers on his desk.

"You don't like him?" I suggest.

"Oh, I like him enough. It's just that he is sort of…*un roué*…a bit cunning, if you know what I mean. Never any money – he uses women for that – drives René crazy – always wanting more money. René thinks he gambles."

"Is he married?"

"Good lord no!" Jean-Luc explodes. "Any woman would be insane to marry such a man."

"Well, in spite of everything, he is attractive in a sly kind of way. Many women are drawn to 'bad boys'."

"You, Madame?" Jean-Luc says in mock horror.

"Not me. Not Monsieur Giscard, Jean-Luc. For me there is Brit and Brit alone. You know that," I say, rising.

"But, of course, Elizabeth," he replies standing. "But you have given me a thought." He has a bright look on his face. "Do you think Bonny Brandeis is a attracted to 'bad boys', *heh?*"

"Wow!" and I plunk down on the chair.

"*Il est tellement séduisant…'le mauvais fils,' Giscard,*" Jean-Luc says, coming toward me around the desk.

"Seductive!" I exclaim. "You can say that again. How brilliant, Jean-Luc! Do you think he would do it?"

"Do exactly what?" he says smiling down at me.

"Seduce Bonny enough to reveal her secrets?"

"*Sans doute, Madame.* There's no question. Giscard can make her reveal everything, much more than her secrets, I can assure you. He can make her fall in love."

"You think?" I exclaim with delight.

"I think!" he says firmly, "and what a *coup!*"

CHAPTER 13

A Naked Maja

IT IS FACING the wall, a small canvas only a foot or so tall. It is half hidden by the corner of Brit's bed.

It is late Friday morning. Last night, Brit and I had dined at *La Cocotte* around the corner from his house, then spent the sweetest kind of lazy evening together. I remained close to him until the sun broke through this morning.

"What's that?" I say, pointing to the picture on the floor. Something new?"

"What?" he says.

"That little painting."

"I have no idea." Brit leans over and turns the picture around. The image, in oil, is of a naked woman.

I am silent. "Who is she?" I manage to say.

"Damned if I know." Brit is looking on the back. "No signature," he mumbles and replaces the offending picture on the floor again, against the wall by the bed as it had been.

I am disturbed. Brit looks preoccupied as we go downstairs. He starts to prepare coffee in a *filter*, as I remove two *croissants* from the bread box to be heated.

As I do, from the corner of my eye, I see, in the salon, under the somewhat threadbare couch, what looks to be a dark green rag. It seems to beckon.

After placing the *croissants* in the warm oven, I go into the next room to the couch and pull forth the rag. Of course, it is not a rag at all. It is a dark green scarf in light cashmere. On one edge, on the inner side, is a tiny, cloth tab with the initials, YSL. I am stunned.

Slowly returning to the kitchen, I approach Brit. "She was here, wasn't she?"

"Who?"

"Bonny Brandeis."

"You know she was. Her umbrella had The Hotel Majestic logo on it. It's how we knew where she was…"

"But she was here again," I interrupt, "wasn't she Brit?" I am trembling.

"As a matter of fact, yes." He is busily pouring coffee. "I didn't want to tell you."

"Why not?"

"I knew it would upset you," and glancing at me, he continues, "and I can see it has."

"I hate secrets," I say, practically falling onto the nearest bentwood chair.

"Look. I couldn't believe that woman in her green dress appearing again at my front door. It was the day you were with the lawyer."

"And this picture?" I say, furious. "This naked picture?"

"It's not mine! That woman must have left it here."

"Oh, Brit. You can do better than that," I say with disgust. I am staggered by the whole concept that he might have been with that woman and painted her nude!

"Look," he says boldly. "She just appeared. Again! I told her to go to the Fernand et Fils Gallery on St. Honoré, because she said 'I want to own a Ludwig Turner painting'. Then she told me, she came to the house because she thought that maybe the large canvasses might be too expensive, and perhaps if I had a drawing or sketch here at my studio that she might like…? 'See I even brought my leather case to take it back to the hotel carefully,' she said, simpering around and so coy…"

"So you let her in," I interrupt.

"Well, sure. Money is money," Brit replies.

I give him a skeptical look.

"Elizabeth, you can't think I'm attracted to that brassy blonde."

"She's got a great figure, and she's young…younger than me."

"Oh, please," he answers angrily. "You think…God, you're exasperating!" and he slaps his brow.

"Methinks the gentleman doth protest too much," I say, sarcastically, and immediately regret saying this. His expression is a mixture of hurt and disbelief.

I rush to him. "I'm so sorry, really sorry, Brit. But, the green scarf on the floor by the couch, the naked woman picture facing the wall…"

"That woman placed those things there. You know she did," he says vehemently. "She must have bought that awful picture at a nearby shop, brought it in the house in her leather case, and placed it facing the wall in my bedroom."

"Your bedroom," I say softly.

"Sure. That's where I keep my folder of sketches and work sheets. Upstairs. She wanted to buy one. Of course, in the end she didn't because she had no intention of doing so. She really wanted to get cozy with me, - I figure that was her real reason for being here - so I brought the folder downstairs, and told her, if there was nothing else…and she finally left, quite morosely, I thought. I tell you, she's a piece of work!"

"She came on to you?" I mumble.

"Yes. I have to say she did. But I want nothing to do with her. She wants to ruin US, Elizabeth, and you in particular. She wants to break us up! That would be even more of a victory for her than screwing up your credit, costing you your savings. It would hurt your heart and she knows it!" He pauses, questioningly. "It would hurt your heart, wouldn't it?"

"Oh God, yes. Oh, Brit, I'd be devastated."

"That's exactly what she wants for you – devastation." And then he added, "It would kill me too."

I am crying, partly because of the realization of her viciousness, partly with relief at his passionate disgust with this woman, this Bonny Brandeis, and partly for his defense of me.

Then we are in each other's arms.

Finally, after many consoling moments and kisses and love words, Brit extricates himself. He runs upstairs, and brings down the offending Naked Maja picture into the kitchen. He studies it intently, then turns to me, "You really think I paint like that?" Brit's sense of insult staggers me. He is angered anew, just by viewing the picture. "Look at me." He is shouting. "You cannot seriously think that a) I cheated on you with that woman, and b) almost as important, that my work is of this caliber!"

He is furious, and I am cowering in some kind of guilty despair. But underneath, secretly, I am ecstatic over the realization that he is absolutely right, that there is no possibility he could have painted this bright blonde-headed, Naked Maja that confronts us, much less taken Bonny Brandeis to the bed in the room upstairs.

It is a small painting, the face of the subject turned away, the body nude and pale, her brilliant blonde hair flowing across one breast, and below as well, at the juncture of her legs. She is lying on a red divan.

"You think I'd put that woman on some sort of crimson damask? Honestly? Elizabeth! This is not my style." He is quite legitimately distraught. "I thought you knew me better than that. I thought we understood each other."

"But she came here to you…"

"And you believed I bought into her wiles? After all the stuff about the credit cards – the stuff about identity theft that you know she's perpetrated against you, you still believed I could sleep with her and do this…this desecration?" and he flings the canvas from him. It lands near the pail for trash.

"I know how disappointed you are in me," I say, dolefully.

He has slowed his pacing and comes to where I sit forlornly on my kitchen chair.

"Sweetheart," he says, leaning down to me. "Are you really so insecure about us?"

With this, I can only look up at him and say, "I guess I find you too good to be true." And he takes me in his arms again, anger forgotten, Bonny Brandeis long disappeared from heart and mind, and it is just Brit and me once again.

CHAPTER 14

A Majestic Suite

ALTHOUGH JEAN-LUC, BRIT and I were obviously not present, in the flesh, for the encounter, Giscard Poignal proved to be quite the narrator of his tryst with Bonny Brandeis, in, frankly, almost too specific detail.

The three of us, Brit, Giscard and myself, are having Sunday morning *café/croissant* at a small restaurant, *Pain et Chocolat,* on an adjoining avenue to Hotel Marcel's.

"By the way, I am meeting with the lady again tomorrow night for a re-encounter. It is then that I will begin to insert the fact that Elizabeth and I had an affair..."

"You've got to be kidding!" I exclaim.

"No, no," Giscard says. "Brit, it's not true. I never met Elizabeth before now." He is looking at Brit whose mouth has dropped. "It's just a way to get the good Bonny to trust me more, to make her think she and I are in collusion against your lady love," and he gives Brit one of his most seductive smiles.

There is no other way but to present here his colorful reconstruction of the Saturday evening when Bonny Brandeis provided a vivid addendum to our entangled destinies.

Giscard finds her in a corner of The Majestic bar. "I am in my black suit and shirt, but with a long white tie that I wear for special occasions," he says, a bit arrogantly.

It is near 6:00 o'clock on Saturday night. Bonny is alone in a rose printed dress with a deep V-neck, a martini with a green olive before her, on the small table. First, Giscard sits at the bar, ordering a martini for himself, also with an olive, sending her side glances, to which she begins to respond.

When his drink is set before him, he turns to her, raises his glass in her direction, and slowly lowers his lips to the rim of the glass, never taking his eyes from hers.

Oh, boy, is he a pro or what! I think. Within seconds, he sees the small curved finger beckoning him to join her at her table. And Giscard does.

It does not take long before she asks him to accompany her to her suite upstairs. "We can order a little personal room service – my treat…" (my treat - two words that are music to Giscard's ears). "I so hate the *ambiance* in the *Fusion* dining room," she says grandly.

"A lovely idea," Giscard agrees, and they are on their way, after, of course, Bonny signs the bar tab.

"I like your style," Giscard says, taking her arm under his, as they cross the lobby with its black and white tile floor, to the bank of elevators.

On gaining the suite, Bonny declares she is not really hungry yet, and let's have another martini, which Giscard shakes up, from the stocked open bar in the salon of the lavish apartment. Taking their stemmed glasses outside to the balcony, they look upon Paris below them in the falling light and pricks of lamps being turned on and streetlights blooming. Touching their glasses, rim to rim, they toast each other.

Giscard leans against the rail of the balcony, his arm about her shoulders, 'against the cold,' he says. "Tell me. How come you are staying in this luxurious place? How lucky can you get?" he says with a smile.

"Lucky indeed," she responds. "I have a benefactor. Oh, it's not what you think," she says coyly, noticing his raised eyebrow. "It's kind of a cause we have – the two of us."

"What kind of cause?"

"Well, it's difficult to say," Bonny responds, taking a long pull at her drink. "It's – well – it's a person – a woman – that we mutually want to…"

"To what?"

"Well, she's done us both wrong. That's all I can say."

"Some sort of vendetta?" Giscard ventures.

"You could say so. And this man," she says, taking another long sip, "well, guess what, he's an Arab sheikh! In fact, he is one of the owners of this hotel."

"So he's bankrolling you here?"

"Well," she says, offended, "if you want to put it that way."

"What would you call it?"

"Hamad needs me here. I have a real purpose for being here," she says defensively.

"How did you meet this Arab sheikh?"

"At a charity event. We danced…had drinks…found we both had a hatred for a particular malicious woman…"

"How did she come up?"

"I don't actually remember – but the point is, she did." Bonny is beginning to feel her drinks. "Whew, I think I'd like to go inside now."

"Okay," and Giscard takes her arm and leads her back to the salon, but Bonny continues walking on, into an adjoining room with its large, handsome, silk-covered bed.

"We met again, Hamad and I, at the place for tea at the Plaza Hotel," Bonny is rattling away. "You know they've kept that room exactly the same– The Palm Court – the new Arab owners have. It's so New York chic! Anyway, I gave Hamad this woman's personal information – you know, Social Security number, credit card number, Savings Bank account number."

"How'd you get all that?" Giscard is by now running a finger down the side of Bonny's neck toward her cleavage, as they lie side by side on the huge Majestic bed.

"Um, Sweetie…I got them off the documents I took from the charity, 'A Child's Voice,' when I left."

"Hmm," Giscard says, his hand closer to her bosom. "Tell me more."

"Well, Hamad decided the woman would buy a house that he saw in Paris that he had wanted. Of course, she would know nothing about it until her money had changed hands. Hamad hated her. Even the whole city of Paris became anathema to him – because of her, and he was determined to ruin her, 'relieve her of sizeable sums,' as he put it. God, he really despises her - almost as much as I do."

"So it was Hamad who put this woman's money down on a Paris house."

"No. No, silly! Hamad had ME go to the Chase bank, and pretend I was her," Bonny says, rising up, restless, snuggling close to Giscard.

"How could you, pretty little Bonny, fool the bank people?" he asks.

"That was easy enough," she says, blushing. "I went to one of the head tellers. They have so many of them. I had all the proper ID numbers - and a transfer by Western Union, $75,000 to put as a good faith down payment on property in Paris, is a simple enough procedure. The money was sent to the realtor Hamad had worked with, a Mme. Toinette Minet who had shown him the house at 13 rue Monsieur…Don't you love the name 'Monsieur', honey," Bonny says, her hand on Giscard's cheek.

He smiles down at her upturned face.

"Apparently, it was a beautiful house, once belonged to Cole Porter, three stories with a garden at the back, super for little dinner parties under the stars." Bonny's face is glowing.

"So the money was sent…" Giscard is now toying with the blonde hair.

"Yeah. Hamad, separately, notified Madame Minet that this woman friend of his, wanted the house desperately and would be in contact. 'She has to have it!' he emailed Toinette, and he had Toinette inform that woman here in Paris, telling her that she had bought a house!" Bonny is laughing raucously. "I'll bet she dropped her teeth when she learned she was out $75,000 in cash!" And Bonny laughs even louder.

"I would guess she was pretty upset," Giscard responds.

"Wouldn't you be?" Hey," Bonny says, sitting up. "Do you know that woman is staying right next door at that tawdry little Hotel Marcel?"

"No!" Giscard exclaims, feigning shock.

"Yes. She's there! Can you believe it? Anyway, like it or not, she's bought herself a house! Pretty slick, no?"

Giscard throws his head back laughing. "I would say so! Pretty slick indeed."

"Why do we have to keep talking about this?" she says petulantly. "It's boring, and I hate her, and enough already."

Giscard laughs again. "Oh no, my dear. We do not have to speak of this any more. Not at all," and he un-loosens the long, white tie. Bonny is now quite beside herself. She touches Giscard's cheek again, then pulls his face to hers.

He decides the moment is ripe and proceeds to do what Giscard is known for and what Giscard does best - throughout the night.

CHAPTER 15

A Secret Weapon

SUE IS ARRANGING for Sasha Goodwin, the American photographer of note, to take photographs of Bonny Brandeis for Paris *Vogue*, this with the special dispensation of Ray Guild, my friend, and Managing Editor of that prestigious magazine. Of course, she has informed both men that we are involved in a sting of sorts against this nefarious woman who is out to ruin Elizabeth.

"No way will she hurt our Elizabeth!" Sasha exclaims. "This Bonny Brandeis will have an elaborate comeuppance, I can guarantee it. Can't wait to catch her at her worst, and believe me, I will."

Sasha, Ray, and I are in the salon of Hotel Marcel. It is early Sunday evening. We await the arrival of the Marquise and Franco, as I fill the two men in on further details of the vendetta Bonny has inflicted on me. They are all sympathy.

Willie Blakely is at the front desk, listening, shaking his head, clucking his teeth. It is late enough that no other clients are in the salon, only Brigitte who is pouring glasses of *Merlot*, and serving wedges of cheese, *baguette*, and *cornichons*. She is one of us, a loyal and true employee of Hotel Marcel.

Through the lobby door, René Poignal arrives with brother, Giscard. We all turn, and wave to them, as they make their way back to Jean-Luc's office.

"Who is that lovely fellow in the black suit?" Ray asks me. "Stunning? Do you suppose he's gay?" this said hopefully.

I have to laugh. "Sorry, Ray dear, but just the opposite. He is our secret weapon – out to seduce the wicked witch next door at The Majestic. He has a reputation of great prowess in that department."

"What a pity," Ray says, with a sigh.

"I must say he's good-looking, in a dirty sort of way," Sasha chimes in.

"Oh, come now, Sasha. He's quite a nice fellow – but, indeed, he may indeed be one of the 'bad boys.' That's why he's perfect for the job we want him to do. Someone like Bonny must find him irresistible," I interject.

With that comment, Sue, La Marquise, with Franco de Peverelli in tow, rush through the lobby door, apologizing for being late, greeting the three of us at table with hugs and hellos.

"It's getting cold out there," Franco says, rubbing his hands together.

"Well, it's warm in here," Sue says, removing her coat and sitting down next to Sasha. "When can we take Bonny's picture?"

Sasha laughs. "You certainly get right to the point, don't you, Madame La Marquise!"

"And why not. We're here on a mission, no?" she answers, laughing with him.

"Whenever you tell me," he says. "I'm there." And he glances at me affectionately.

Before Sue and Franco have a chance to sip their wine, Jean-Luc, René, and Giscard join us at the long table. Introductions are made. Sue slips next to me. "Man oh man, He is *quelque chose, non?*" she whispers, referring to Giscard's dark, good looks. "He is as emotionally lethal as a loaded gun," I whisper back, and then the two of us are all smiles and chitchat for the moment, as we prepare to make some decisions in the matter of the fate of Bonny Brandeis.

"Why can't we photograph her now?" Sasha asks, grinning. "No time like the present."

"You might find her a bit disheveled," Giscard says with a mischievous grin. "She and I...well, we were very busy."

"Aha," says Ray. "All the better. We will tell her, of course, that the picture will be for the article in *Vogue* on American women who do not live in Paris but adore the city and want to do things for it. That will mean she will have to make a contribution to a Paris institution – From Bonny Brandeis! – in large letters. Do you think she'll go for it?" Ray says, turning his full attention on Giscard.

"She's always got Hamad to back her... Besides, she has me, and I will see that she does," Giscard says with another sly smile.

"I'm going to call her this minute," Sue says, reaching for her purse, removing her cell phone and quickly dialing.

"Suite 555," we hear her say. There is a pause. Then, "Bonny darling. It's your new friend Sue de Chevigny." Another pause. "Look, I am not far away with the people from *Vogue* – the Managing Editor and his best photographer, and they would so much appreciate being able to do a photo shoot."

We hear bright girlish sounds from the phone, as Sue continues. "Well, right now."

More peals of sound from the phone, agitated, high-pitched.

"No matter, darling Bonny. These men are pros. They know exactly what to do to put you together for the perfect *Vogue* (Sue's voice is very emphatic!) photograph. Leave it up to them. Now, now, I can assure you they will know exactly how to dress you. Not to worry. I am telling you, these are real professionals." There is another pause, and silence from the phone. "Can we come up?" Sue asks sweetly.

With a nod to the interested faces at the table, Sue rings off and with a radiant smile, she says, "Come on fellas, let's go! We've got a job to do."

Giscard stands. "I think perhaps it's best if I do not join you," he says. "I want to keep the *mystique* at full height, her anticipation whetted. Don't you agree?"

"You mean this is all too *mondain?*" Jean-Luc queries.

"Exactly. I want to keep things uncertain, a bit off balance," Giscard says. "We are to meet again in her suite tomorrow evening…" He pauses, a weighted moment, full of innuendo. "I don't want to take the edge off that moment by appearing now. Let her wait." Then, without any pride, Giscard continues, "I know exactly what I'm doing, and frankly, it's intriguing and great fun." I feel a chill as he says these things.

I look at him and decide at that moment that Giscard Poignal is indeed a 'bad boy'. He does not really love women, as I had thought. He loves to use them. He delights in bringing them to heights, than dropping them low.

Suddenly, I think, 'poor Bonny', then 'no, Bonny isn't poor at all.' That woman deserves exactly what this man is able to dish out – ecstasy for a while – a broken heart and spirit for the rest.

Bonny has surely met her match!

CHAPTER 16

In Vogue

LATER, THIS SUNDAY evening, Brit joins me from his house in the Marais. We wait in the salon of the Hotel Marcel for the return of Sue, Franco, Ray Guild and Sasha Goodwin from their mission next door at The Majestic Hotel suite 555 of Bonny Brandeis. Brit and I sit close, his hand in mine, under the table.

Giscard and René Poignal, as well as Jean-Luc, are here too, polishing off another bottle of *Merlot* and more cheese and *baguette*. Dinner is long forgotten. We are eager to learn the results of the photo shoot in Bonny's aerie above the avenue.

It is near 10:00 o'clock. It has been a long evening. We are all tired, practically nodding off, Brit and I eager to be off to my balconied room on the 5th floor, when we hear excited voices, sounds of laughter and bustle, as our four friends appear from the cold outside. They are animated, humorous, with an air of victory emanating from all four of them.

"More wine," Jean-Luc calls to Willie Blakely who has emerged from his bed downstairs in the basement area.

Willie shuffles to the back kitchen and retrieves three bottles, this time, *Pinot Noir*, an equally delicious red, that he pours all round, setting extra glasses before Sue, Franco, Ray, and Sasha.

"Tell us. Tell us," I say, rousing up.

"You wouldn't believe it," Franco says, sitting down next to me, taking a large sip of his red wine. "In the first place, she looked kind of blousy..."

"She explained that she hadn't had time to dress," Sue interrupts. "She was in this kind of chemise – and my God, her hair was all over the place. I think the poor thing was really kind of embarrassed."

"And no one had cleaned the room," Sasha says.

"Well, it is Sunday," I chime in.

"But in a five star hotel?" Sasha shakes his head. "Anyway, I find a terry robe in the bathroom. Ray starts brushing her hair. I sit her on a divan, wrapped in the robe, and take some pictures. She looks like a caricature of Marilyn Monroe."

"In the meantime," Sue says, Franco is telling her that, in order to be part of the article, she must contribute to a Paris charity of some sort. I suggest the children's hospital, but Bonny turns up her nose at that, saying somewhat bitterly, I thought, 'I've had that drink!' I suppose referring to 'A child's Voice.'"

"'What about the American Library in Paris,' Ray then suggested to her. 'It has a nice intellectual touch, don't you think?'"

"I thought that was brilliant," Sue says to us. Ray looks pleased. "And Bonny? She got all excited. 'Yes, yes,' she said. 'How much should I give'? and I said, 'Oh, at least $10,000 - of course in euros' at which Bonnie looked a bit surprised."

"She was appalled," Sasha interrupts with a laugh.

"Anyway, once we get the 10K for the Library," Ray says, I will have to tell her that the whole article has been cancelled."

"On what grounds?" I ask.

"Oh, I guess because not enough American women in Paris came forward. Can't have an article with only two or three. I'll think of something," Ray finishes.

Giscard has been sitting there, drinking his wine, silent. There is an amused look on his face. "A caricature of Marilyn Monroe," he says. "You know, that is perfect…Bonny Brandeis, the ersatz Monroe. Well, my friends, I certainly have my work cut out for me tomorrow night. It should be a blast. I'd better get some rest."

"While your at it," I say, blushing. "I mean while you are in her suite, do you think you could look for her new credit card? It has MY name on it!"

"Your name? How come?"

"It's a long story," I say, "but the point is, she has been buying stuff, trying to ruin me…"

"Enough said," Giscard says gallantly. "I will do my best to retrieve it for you, Elizabeth."

"She would be most grateful," Brit chimes in, uncomfortable when this man is around.

"Consider it done," Giscard says, getting up and leaving the table to walk upstairs to his little room on the 3rd floor of the Hotel Marcel. As he does so, over his shoulder, he says, "Jean-Luc, I'll be checking out in the morning. After tonight, any of you can find me next door in suite 555."

CHAPTER 17

Re-Entry In Suite 555

AT TUESDAY'S LATE breakfast, again at *Pain et Chocolat*, Brit and I, lingering over the specialty of the place, steaming hot chocolate with whipped cream, await the arrival of Giscard. We prepare ourselves for the recitation of gory details of his night with Bonny Brandeis we expect to be privy to, that frankly, I am eager to hear.

He comes swinging through the door to the little restaurant, neat as a pin. His black suit and shirt, white tie, look crisp and pressed. He sits down with a morning smile and asks the waiter for *'un café noir, s'il vous plaît.'*

"Well, Giscard," Brit says, not quite knowing how to start this intimate conversation.

"Eh bien," Giscard responds. "It has been quite an evening...quite a night with, as Sasha put it, the caricature of Marilyn Monroe. Yes, indeed." His coffee appears and he tests its heat with his lips. As he does so, he pulls a small article from his pocket and places it carefully in front of me without a word.

I look down. It is Bonny Brandeis new Master Card with my name imprinted on it, new numbers, expiration date, security number on the back. I grab it, clutching it to my chest. "Oh Giscard! Thank you."

"At least you're solvent again," he says.

"How did you manage to get it?"

"When the lady went to the john. Her purse was right there on the table. I slipped it from her wallet. Easy as pie," he says, ordering another *café* from the hovering waiter.

"God, I am so grateful. I can't tell you. She won't be able to run up a huge tab any more, at least for the moment. Did you learn more of her plots?" I ask. "Any new schemes up her sleeve?"

"Not exactly," he replies. "But I have set up quite a little plot of my own." He takes a long pull at the coffee cup. He notices the look of alarm on my face, "Oh, not against you, Elizabeth. Against the good Bonny."

"What kind of plot?" Brit is perplexed.

"I asked her to marry me."

"What?" I say with a laugh. "You're not serious!"

Giscard shakes his head. "Of course not, but she bought it."

"Really. But so soon?" We are all laughing now. "For God's sake, what did she say?" I inquire.

"She's ecstatic, of course," Giscard says with a smile.

"How did this all come about?"

"Well, we met downstairs in the bar as agreed. Then, martini time. Then up to the suite. No dinner of course. Right to the bedroom."

"No amenities, I see," Brit says with a chuckle.

"Hardly," Giscard says. "Bonny was…I don't know how to put it… quite desperate…I guess, hungry, is the better word – but not for supper."

I realize I am blushing.

"After…an amount of time, and you know…after all the…goings on, she's tired, and 'had to catch her breath', as she put it – and well, we talked a little, and then she told me there had been a photo shoot, that she might be on the cover of *Vogue* magazine."

"Lord she must have been all puffed up with that idea," Brit remarked.

"Oh, she was," Giscard went on. "She did mention she would have to make a sizeable donation to the American Library – and I suggested, Hamad would pay for it, and she said, of course, he will have to. 'I have no money' she said. I didn't tell her – 'don't ask me for it because neither do I'." And Giscard started to laugh.

So did Brit and I – nervously.

"I then asked Bonny why she had never told me the name of this terrible person, this woman, and she said she had trusted no one – not even me – until now."

"Did she tell you?"

"Yes. She blurted out your name, Elizabeth."

"And?" I'm about to jump out of my skin.

"I sat right up in bed, got to my feet, and said, 'not her! Not Elizabeth!' And Bonny screamed, 'you know her?' and I said, 'not only do I know her, she wanted to marry me!'"

"What?" I am really laughing now. All three of us are. We order more chocolate and coffee. Brit and I sit there with our fists under our chins, elbows on the table, as Giscard continues.

"'What do you mean Elizabeth wanted to marry you?' Bonny went on and on, and I told her, 'yes, she did…we had an affair and…'"

"'You had an affair with that woman? You asked her to marry you?' she ranted. I said I hadn't asked Elizabeth to marry me. She had asked me, at which Bonny calmed down and with a smug look on her face, said 'well, you didn't. Of course not, you couldn't marry that woman!' and I replied, 'no I didn't want to. It wasn't like you, Bonny, and me.'" Giscard pauses, takes a slow drink of coffee, lights a cigarette.

"Then what happened?" I whisper.

"She suddenly got very coy, very clingy. 'Giscard,' she said. 'You and I…well, it's different. What we have…'and I told her I agreed, that perhaps the two of us, one day… and she said 'why one day? Why not soon?' and she was all over me again…reaching…"

"Okay, Okay, Giscard. Enough detail," Brit interrupts. "How did you leave it with her?"

"Huh," Giscard says, inhaling smoke from his cigarette deeply. "I dangled the idea of marriage in front of her...teased her with it - but I said that things had happened between us so quickly – and she comes back with 'that's when one knows. When it's quick, immediate. One knows at once!' She was so...so...convinced. So I pretended to agree with her."

You bastard, I thought, but then, Giscard was being a bastard with Bonny Brandeis, so that makes it okay!

"Hey, Giscard," Brit says, with a twinkle. "You can have the wedding at Sue's *château*. That will put the bride over the moon."

"She already is," Giscard says with a laugh. "And hey, you know the *château's* not a bad idea!"

"You're not serious?" I say. The thought is appalling.

"Hardly! I have no intention of doing anything with Bonny Brandeis other than..."

"Don't say it," Brit interrupts.

"It's my *forté*, Giscard declares. "I like to practice my craft."

"I thought your craft is welding?" I say.

His response? "Same difference," with one of those Giscard smiles.

CHAPTER 18

A Gathering Storm

SO THERE IS to be a wedding! (Of sorts). Bonny Brandeis and one devilishly seductive man: Giscard Poignal!

So different from Isabella and Jean-Luc's! So extreme as compared to Lilith and Duke Davis'!

It will be a fiasco that Bonny Brandeis will never forget.

Or forgive.

On this Wednesday morning, over *café au lait,* in the salon of the Hotel Marcel, I ruminate on my state of affairs. I am deeply concerned not only about my credit rating, but more importantly, about the loss of $75,000 in a fraudulent down-payment on a house in Paris I neither need nor want! However, I do realize I am in the excellent hands of Monsieur Jacques Ballon, Jean-Luc's personal attorney.

As the Bonny-sting is set in motion, with Giscard as key player, Sue and Franco in tandem to protect my interests, and of course, Jean-Luc and Isabella as general morale-boosters, Jacques Ballon is in the process of preparing a lawsuit against Bonny Brandeis.

He has in his possession the credit card receipt, with my forged signature, for the green dress and scarf purchased at Yves St. Laurent. Isabella has been able to retrieve it and present it to the goodly lawyer.

Ballon also has the new Master Card that Bonny has acquired in my name that Giscard purloined from her purse. Finally, he has arranged for an appointment with the realtor, Toinette Minet for tomorrow morning, at which we hope to retrieve the $75,000 cash transfer fraudulently obtained by Bonny, from my account at Chase Bank in New York City.

I realize I have to take some responsibility for my predicament; carelessness! In the records of "A Child's Voice" charity, my Social Security Number and credit card number are, of course, no longer still inscribed, nor is my Chase Bank account number. When I resigned as president a year ago, I made sure that all delicate information was deleted from the various files and documents.

However, Bonny had already taken copies of these, with live numbers on them on her escape to Florida, six years earlier, of which theft no one at the charity was aware – least of all myself.

There is no one in this world who could have had access to my sensitive information, except someone at "A child's Voice," and of all people, with Bonny's animosity toward me, who would steal it, who would wish to see me suffer other than Bonny Brandeis?

Even Brit, who I trust implicitly, even he, does not have access to my personal information. It is nobody's business but mine.

Until now, until Bonny Brandeis, out of the past, has raised the ugly face of fraud and identity theft. And I am left to deal with her, but thank God, not alone.

CHAPTER 19

Toinette Minet, Realtor

SHE IS A small-boned woman of a certain age, with black hair cut close to the head, dressed in a smart, understated coffee-colored suit. All I can think of is a small bird, a little brown wren, except her wide mouth outlined in deep red lipstick, the snapping dark eyes, bespeak of a more aggressive creature.

Jacques Ballon, Esq., Jean-Luc and myself have reached Toinette Minet's Realty at the appointed time – 10.00 AM, on Thursday. The receptionist, a young man, asks us to wait, which we do for only a moment, when Toinette herself, opens the door to her inner office and beckons us to come in. Here, she greets us warmly in a kind of bastard English, ushers us to seats facing her desk, and proceeds to congratulate me on my purchase.

"It is such a …lovely house, Madame. You will be very happy there… It needs very little *renouvellements*…"

"Renovations," Jean-Luc whispers to me, at which I glare at him.

"One moment, Madame Minet," I interrupt. "There has been a great mistake made. In fact, a fraud."

"*Une fraude?* Madame. What do you say?" The bird-like face is contorted in disbelief. "How can that be? I have your deposit... all in good faith," and she shuffles papers in the folder on her desk to find a note from Chase Bank, showing the transfer of my money – in the amount of $75,000 – as down payment on the house at 13 rue Monsieur – now deposited in Credit Suisse, Paris.

"This is all perfectly correct, Madame," Toinette says angrily.

"Madame," Jacques Ballon exclaims. "It is not correct.

Ce n'est pas légal. Pas de tout."

"*Pas légal?*" Toinette's face has turned quite white.

"Madame Elizabeth in no way authorized the transfer of funds. Her information – the number of her bank account, her credit card, her social security number – all had been stolen."

"*Impossible!*" the realtor explodes.

"*Non. Non, pas de tout.*" Jacques continues. I am impressed with his firmness. "Why, Madame Elizabeth has never even seen the house at 13 rue Monsieur, now have you?" he says, turning to me.

"I don't even know where rue Monsieur is," I say as strongly as I can. "I have no need nor desire for a house in Paris – much less one I have never laid eyes on."

Toinette looks confused. Jacques translates what I have said. She sits back in her leather chair. "*Je ne comprends pas.*"

"I don't blame you, Madame," Jacques continues in a most placating tone. "*C'est une attrape* - a hoax – perpetrated against my client, Madame Elizabeth, and we, as proper French citizens, must honor her claim. You must return the money to her, *immédiatement,*" at which Toinette's face turns even whiter.

"I was assured," Toinette begins, in a tremulous voice, "by none other than Hamad al-Boudi himself, that Madame Elizabeth was determined to obtain the house on rue Monsieur, that she was particularly *excité* by the fact it had belonged to Cole Porter, the musician *tellement fameux...*"

"That's ridiculous, Madame Minet," I say vehemently. "I knew absolutely nothing about this whole...this whole monkey business..."

"Monkey business?" she asks. "What is monkey business?"

"This *farce*," Jean-Luc says helpfully.

"*Oh, mon Dieu*," she says with a sigh. "*Eh bien*, Madame. Perhaps now you would like to see the house for your own appraisal," this said with a big smile. "It is truly a little *bijou*..."

"I don't care if it's the biggest *bijou* in *tout Paris*. I am not buying a house under any circumstances."

"You don't wish to see it?" she persists with the insinuating smile.

"No," I say. "All I want is my money back."

"And that shall be arranged, Madame Minet. That shall be arranged right here and right now," Jacques Ballon intervenes with a smile equal to Toinette's.

And in fact, it IS arranged. Jacques Ballon, Esq. remains at the realtor's office, after I sign a specific document that he has prepared in advance. I am assured the $75,000 will be returned to my account in New York, "minus a small transfer fee," Toinette says, with a deprecating *mou*.

Jean-Luc and I find a taxi at a nearby stand. We settle back happily in the rear of the vehicle. I look over at my friend, as he says to me, with a rakish smile, "You really don't want to see a house on rue Monsieur?"

"No, no, Monsieur. Who needs a house in Paris when there's always the Hotel Marcel!" I exclaim, as the taxi whirls through the Paris streets, traversing in the absolutely right direction!

CHAPTER 20

Les Preparations

ON REACHING MY room on the 5th floor of Hotel Marcel, I call Sue and describe my visit with Toinette Minet.

"Thank heavens for the lawyer. Do you really think you'll get your money back?"

"He assures me that I will."

Sue, delighted with the whole scheme of things, is in her element arranging for a wedding at *Le Couvent* on the coming Sunday.

"So soon," she exclaims. "It's already Thursday and Sunday seems only minutes away, but frankly, I am thrilled that this whole Bonny-thing is reaching its *dénouement*.

"My God, it is quick," I say, "but I'm sure Giscard is ready to get the whole thing over and done with."

"I'll just bet. Bonny must be a quite a handful to take, over time."

"Even 'bed' can become onerous," I say.

"For Giscard?" Sue says with a laugh. "There, I imagine he could go on forever. It's the other Bonny 'attributes" that can be truly hard to bear."

"You can say that again."

"We haven't had so much excitement in years," Sue says happily on the phone. "I already have some women in the village pressing the linen for the dining room. I also arranged for a huge cake to be baked at Montoire's best bakery. Franco is preparing some bottles from our own winery, although the grape juice is still young and a bit raw – but he is thrilled to be able to display his works of art."

"But you realize, Sue," I interject, "that there will actually be no wedding. In fact, the groom has already purchased his one-way, single train ticket for Barcelona for that very day."

"He's not going to show up?"

"Of course not. He has no intention of taking this *charade* with Bonny any further."

"My God! Bonny will be in shock!" Sue pauses. I can almost hear my friend thinking. "But we can still have a party, no?"

"By all means. A celebration. By the way, René Poignal is to be the best man. He plans to take the bride away with him, back to the Paris jail!"

"It may sound cruel," Sue says with a laugh, "but what a way to end a party! *Quel sommet!*"

"*Quel sommet?* What's that?"

"It means, what a climax! I guess that's the best word. Yes, my dear, Bonny will have the climax of her life! And a honeymoon behind bars."

CHAPTER 21

Face En Face

IT WAS BOUND to happen. Bonny with her intensely passionate love with Giscard, and with a newfound sense of entitlement, decides it is time to face the lion - me – in my lair. In other words, she has come to the lowly Hotel Marcel, empowered, eager to cut me to ribbons and show her superiority.

"I have been waiting for this moment. I've been waiting lo these six years." Bonny's eyes flash as she speaks, her mouth contorted.

She has found me finally. She has had the gall to come to my room on the 5th floor. It is near noon on Friday. There is a tap on my door, and there she stands; Bonny Brandeis, in a bright orange suit.

My bedroom is small, now filled with a woman in towering anger, and me, trying to control myself, not to give away any sense of secrets to come.

"When I left 'A Child's Voice,' I was so pissed," she says in a loud voice. "I wanted to write a note to you – a funeral note on paper lined with black."

"Why didn't you?"

"I didn't want to prepare you for this day," she says sarcastically. "I would have declared 'I will never forget you, Elizabeth – what you did to me, how you ruined my life. There will come a day!' I would have written, and by God, that day is come! We are here. We are now. Just how does it feel?" Bonny says, moving towards me, as I stand near the glass doors to the balcony. I am as impassive as I can be.

"You have no idea," she says, bending toward me. "The years in Florida – wasted years – married to a 'retiree', a dull man. At least he had a swimming pool."

"Why didn't you stay put?" I ask.

"I told you. He was dull! I was bored to death. Then came along a guy in P.R. – pretty well known in New York City for his sharpness. He was just a tourist, but after we met, he came down to Boca all the time for what he called, 'some of that special Florida sea food'! ME!" She smiles smugly. "Yeah. We were great in the sack."

"Good for you," I say sarcastically. "One of your great talents, eh?"

"You could say so." Bonny is pacing around the bed. "You ruined my life for so many years. I decided that one day, I would do the same to you. And I have, haven't I," she says triumphantly.

"Have what?"

"Ruined your life."

As I make no response, she continues. "It all came together just recently, my plans for you. I got back to New York with my P.R. guy..."

"He hasn't a name?" I say pointedly.

"Doesn't matter. Listen to me, Elizabeth." Bonny's tone is nasty. "I'm talking to you – about you – and my success in destroying who you think you are!"

I cringe at the menace in her voice. But Bonny is not through. She has saved the best for last.

"Yes, indeed! I've ruined your credit! Nobody trusts you any more. And best of all, I've ruined your romance with that guy Brit."

"Brit?" My heart freezes. "You know about Brit?" I ask, voice quavering, consciously egging her on.

"Oh sure. Hamad al-Boudi was just full of information – couldn't stop talking about your artist accomplice helping his daughter defect."

"Hamad al-Boudi?" I say, pretending I know nothing of their collusion. "What's he got to do with you?"

"That's my business," she says haughtily.

"And Brit wasn't an accomplice," I say, feebly.

"Who cares," Bonnie says. "Ah, yes, Brit. He is attractive, you know. I went over there with the excuse of seeing his paintings."

I say nothing. The first time she had come to the house in the Marais on the pretense of buying a picture, we learned Bonny's whereabouts – that she had a suite at the Majestic. Next, of course, there had been her Naked Maja picture ploy, and the green scarf.

She walks around me, eyeing me. "He was very receptive, your Brit," she says, her voice filled with sarcasm. "But, it wasn't hard to get to him, you know. After all, I'm quite a bit younger than you," she says, cruelly. "And by the way, your Brit, he, too, thinks I'm great in the sack."

Seeing me wince, she continues her verbal attack, pacing, circling me, moving close. "Did he tell you about that?"

"You're lying," I manage to say.

"No, of course he wouldn't tell you," she says. "Ask him! Ask your precious Brit." She has picked up her handbag, and is heading for the door. "Oh yes, Elizabeth. Just ask Brit how he couldn't wait to paint me… of course in the nude. I guess that goes with the territory!"

"Oh, yes Bonny. I will surely ask him," (but of course I already have).

"Perhaps he'll let you see his latest work of art." As Bonny leaves, she calls over her shoulder, "I'm off to Yves to buy me a dress for a wedding at a *château!*" and she slams the door behind her.

With what credit card, I think. Doesn't she realize that her new one is missing?

I am pleased with myself. I have withstood the diatribe. I am quite elated in fact. Bonny hasn't a clue that Brit has leveled with me, what he really thinks of her, and most important, she hasn't the least idea of what is to befall her.

A marriage to Giscard Poignal! A wedding in a *château!*

Ah, yes, Bonny. Dreams can come true, but, I'm afraid, not in your case, my friend. Your bubble is about to burst, and none of us can wait to witness the explosion.

The sting is well in motion, and tomorrow is another day.

But Bonny is still not finished.

Willie Blakely calls from the front desk late Friday afternoon, to say that a visitor was on the way up to my room to see me.

"Brassy looking woman, Madame Elizabeth. Not your type. I think she is the culprit. She was here yesterday...the same one."

At least I am warned. I am prepared.

"With all the satisfaction I feel in getting back at you, Elizabeth, nothing can compare with the thrill of Giscard!" This is her opening salvo.

"I'm sure," I say, through compressed lips.

"What a man – like no other. He barely needs to touch me...and when he does... Well... Thank goodness, suite 555 has solid walls..." and she laughs loudly.

"Do I have to hear all your gory details, Bonny? Too much information...but then you were never known to have any class."

"That's a lie."

"No...no class at all. All your dirty little details. You know, you're an out and out crook, and embezzler, not only from me, but from a children's charity, yet – for your own enrichment!"

"You bitch!" Bonnie shrieks. She is pacing, then turning to me with a victorious smile, she exclaims, "You're just jealous. I am being married on Sunday to a gorgeous man and you ...you are fooling around with an aging artist in his dismal little house..."

"You know something?" I say, standing and facing her. I can't help myself. "I'll just bet your Giscard has a little surprise for you."

"What do you mean?"

"Why don't you wait and see," I say. We are nose to nose.

"The man is crazy for me," she says, swinging away from me. "You have no idea! Well, how would you?" and she looks at me disparagingly.

"Any surprise from Giscard will be welcomed with open arms. He can't get enough of me…oh, but you wouldn't possibly understand."

⊠　⊠　⊠

Later, in the afternoon, when I describe the scene to Giscard Poignal, he is annoyed. "Just what did you say to her?"

"I just told her she might be in for a surprise, from you," I say, meekly.

"Why did you do that? Don't you know I'm trying to inflate her to such a degree, that when she bursts, she'll burst for all time! Don't warn her, Elizabeth, please!"

"I won't. I promise," I say contritely.

"After all, it will all be over soon. We don't want to spoil her unraveling, now do we?" and Giscard gives me that smile. "'Course, I won't be around to see it. I'll be rocking away on the night train south."

Good luck, 'bad boy,' I think. I guess I owe you a thank you, but somehow, I feel an uncharacteristic burst of pity for Bonny Brandeis.

It only lasts a moment.

CHAPTER 22

Frustration

"I TRIED TO buy a wedding dress at Yves St. Laurent. I wanted something fresh and pretty for the momentous occasion, but can you believe it? I couldn't!" Bonny looks ready to break into tears. "Giscard, my new Master Card was missing. Where could it have gone? I know I had it – right there in the wallet in my purse."

"I have no idea, my dear. Perhaps it dropped from your wallet when you were paying the taxi."

"I was furious. They wouldn't let me take the beautiful cream-colored dress I had picked out, even though I promised to get the money to them on Monday. I even tried to reach Hamad at the Plaza Hotel in New York – but he was in Washington, DC for the weekend. I know I could get the price from him – but it would be a day late anyway," she says sadly. "I so wanted our day to be perfect," her visage mournful.

"Ah, my dear, it will be, and you will look lovely in whatever you wear," Giscard says.

"I wish I could come to you in the salon of the *château, au naturel,*" Bonny says coyly.

"There'll be plenty of time for that," Giscard responds turning away, suddenly aware of just how traumatic his absence will be at the moment of truth. However, he is not a man to feel guilt. He is not one to rue his misdeeds. After all, the Bonny venture has been a *cause célèbre* to save Elizabeth from rack and ruin, hasn't it? And frankly, he thinks, the mission will be accomplished, *n'importe quoi.*

On Saturday afternoon, over *aperitifs* and *gougères chez* Jean-Luc and Isabella's apartment, Brit and I hear the story of 'the wedding dress.'

At Yves, this very Saturday morning, Isabella is called down from upstairs in the atelier by a clerk on the first floor, to address an irate woman who wants a dress but has no credit card. "She says she can't find her credit card, but she had bought with it at the couturier's house last week and signed for the dress, and insists on being able to get the outfit she has picked out for her wedding next day. I don't know how to handle her, Isabella. Help. 'There must be a record, a receipt – where you can see my signature', she keeps shouting."

"Of course, it is Elizabeth's name forged on the receipt," Isabella tells us.

Isabella had then descended and explained to Bonny Brandeis that even though there is a record of a previous purchase, the receipt itself is long gone, and it is impossible to let the woman remove a garment from Yves St. Laurent until it is paid for. "That is a hard and fast rule of the establishment," Isabella explained to the visibly distraught woman before her.

"Bonny was beside herself," Isabella exclaims to us as we munch on the delicious cheese puffs and drink *kir royales.*

"I can believe it," Brit says with a laugh. "Our Bonny is something of an outsize nutcase. Did Elizabeth tell you how horrible she was, going up to Elizabeth's room and confronting her with all sorts of accusations?"

"No," says Jean-Luc. "What a virago! You know, I happened to run into Sylvie LaGrange…"

"Another virago," I interject ruefully.

"That she is," Jean-Luc says with a laugh. "She was with Guillaume Paxière…again…"

"That's surely an on-again-off-again *affaire*," I say, laughing too.

"They had plenty to say about your credit card rejection at *Fusion* the other night that they were very busy observing."

"Oh?" I find I am blushing.

Jean-Luc continues. "They even had the gall to ask me if Elizabeth could pay her bill at my hotel! Can you imagine? What nerve."

"And how uncouth to approach you in that way, Jean-Luc," Brit says.

"Oh, I told them as much — that it was in the first place none of their business, and in fact, Madame Elizabeth who has come to my place for over 30 years, always pays in full, and leaves rather grand *pourboires* for my employees."

"*Pourboires?*" I ask. "'For drinks'?"

Jean-Luc tosses his head, really laughing. "*Pourboires* means 'tips'. But the actual translation is a great idea! Let's all have another," and he rises, takes our glasses and proceeds to recreate the elegant *kir royales* for all.

We sip and toast each other and have the most amazing time of friendship possible.

Tomorrow is the 'wedding of the century' we are attending at Sue's *château*. Underneath the intimacy of the moment, there is a *frisson* of anticipation. How will it all play out?

I can't wait.

CHAPTER 23

Preamble

IT IS A frosty October morning, the wedding day of Giscard Poignal and Bonny Brandeis. It is to take place at La Marquise Sue de Chevigny's *château* in Montoire, a couple of hour's drive south, from Paris. The ceremony is scheduled for 4:00 o'clock this Sunday afternoon, to be followed by a small reception.

Jean-Luc has arranged to pick up Jacques Ballon, Esq., midday. Isabella is driving down with Sasha, Ray Guild and Willie Blakely, the latter to preside over service at the reception. Brit and I are ensconced in his Peugeot.

The eight of us plan to meet at a well-known restaurant, *Le Chat Rouge*, in Ambloy, a town about 10 kilometers from Montoire and the *château*. We can have a leisurely lunch before the main event at *le Couvent*. Although in separate vehicles, we are all bubbling with excitement.

René Poignal, the best man for his brother Giscard, will arrive directly at the *château* later in the afternoon. The bride, Bonny Brandeis, has ordered a car and driver to bring her to her groom at Sue's, just in time for the ritual. She has chosen to make her grand entrance solo because, as she tells Giscard, "Can't see you on the wedding day…it's bad luck!" to which he responds, "So you're superstitious, my dear?" and she answers, "Well, I guess I am," and his reply, "Perhaps you should be," which left her a bit confused.

But nothing could touch her joy, this day.

As far as Giscard Poignal, the groom, is concerned, he has no intention whatever of appearing at *Le Couvent*. In fact, he is making his way to a train at the Gare Montparnasse, headed for southwestern France and the Pyrenees, and from there, to Barcelona. His departure happens at the very moment our entourage leaves the city of Paris, in a series of motorcars, on the trip to Montoire.

We arrive, one after the other, in Ambloy. *Le Chat Rouge* is a charming inn off the main street of the town, set back, with a gravel path leading to the front entrance. The place is known for its small, organic chickens, cooked on a rotisserie, with fresh thyme leaves and lemon in the interior of each bird, aromatic additions that permeate the flesh.

Two tables are pulled together, before a large fireplace with glowing coals, to accommodate the eight of us. The chickens are ordered, along with a potato *sauté*, as well as chilled bottles of *champagne*.

After all, we <u>are</u> about to attend a wedding! (Of sorts!)

The chatter at the table is spirited. Sasha announces he has brought his best camera for the event. Ray Guild says how disappointed he is that Giscard will be absent.

"He's so fine to look at," he exclaims. "Careful, now," Sasha says, giving Ray a look. "Not for you, baby," and the two men grin at each other in understanding. They have been associated for a long time, these two, the one living the gay life, the other athletically heterosexual. Sasha just can't resist those models. (Neither can Ray, but models of his own persuasion).

As we savor the delicious food, the fresh bread, the cool wine, Brit asks Jean-Luc, "Who is the prelate at the ceremony?" Then he pauses to think. "Or is there one?"

"I have no idea," Jean-Luc says with a raised eyebrow. "Do you suppose Sue found a religious to perform a fake ceremony – with a missing groom? I would doubt it."

"Well, we shall see soon enough," Brit says with a laugh, then sobering quickly. "You know, I am beginning to feel sorry for the bride."

"Poor Bonny Brandeis," echoes Jacques Ballon. "But after all. Look what she has tried to do to Elizabeth."

"Yes," Isabella responds. "She deserves no pity, no pity at all, now does she!"

CHAPTER 24

A Wedding Belle

SHE ARRIVES! THE town car pulls up to the grand entrance of *Le Couvent*, and out steps Bonny Brandeis, the bride, resplendent in the infamous green Yves St. Laurent sheath. She is wearing a large corsage of white gardenias at her shoulder, and carries a small bouquet of the same fragrant blooms, which she purchased from The Majestic Hotel florist, (on Hamad al-Boudi's hotel bill).

The reason she seems particularly resplendent is because she is highly made up, with truly long black eyelashes attached to her own, and blood red lipstick. Her cheeks are rosy and the blonde hair is piled high with a diamond tiara-like object affixed among the curls. No modest veil for this one, and as Sasha once described her, she is a 'real caricature of Marilyn Monroe'. And indeed, so she appears on this cloudy, Sunday afternoon in October.

Sue opens the massive door to the entry room of the *château* with its high ceilings and tall front windows. To the rear of the room, the guests are clustered like a bunch of flowers. Sue has placed a bank of tall vases of white lilies on the left side at the front of the entry hall.

With a hand over her eyes, Bonny looks with anticipation at those gathered near the inner salon door. She first catches sight of Isabella, standing in a red dress near a high brocade chair. The bride-to-be's look is one of disbelief. To see the sales woman from Yves St. Laurent here and now and why here? makes Bonny's nose twitch.

Her dismay increases as she spots Brit and then me. She lets out a gasp, as she sees the two of us, holding hands, next to Isabella. Her head swings from side to side as she notices Jean-Luc from the paltry Hotel Marcel, and then a fattish gentleman in a plaid vest (Monsieur Ballon). She sees the *Vogue* editor and his photographer, camera in hand. At least, there will be sumptuous pictures! For this, and only for this, Bonny is pleased. And the groom? Perhaps he is superstitious too, but it is the here and now. The moment has arrived. Where is Giscard?

Yet Elizabeth! Why is SHE here? Why is she to be present at such a moment, to spoil the perfection of the day? How and who would have asked her to join the celebration. Giscard? Impossible! The Marquise? Well, she did say she knew Elizabeth, but from Sue's remarks, Bonny assumed the Marquise and Elizabeth are not the greatest of friends.

(Wrong!)

Bonny steps forward, somewhat tentatively. Sasha has already taken a picture or two, saying, "Bonny, turn your head a little to the right. That's it." and "Can you stand there by the lilies? Ah, good. That's good." For this process, Bonny is gracious and poses happily. She is, for the moment, in her element.

Sue lets this last as long as possible, not knowing exactly how to continue. She decides to beckon one and all into the salon – and to the bar table – laden with every conceivable potion – from the new *Le Couvent* wines, to whiskey and gin and, of course, two silver ice buckets with bottles of *champagne*. Willie Blakely is behind the bar table with a big grin on his face. He is ready and waiting to dispense drinks.

Ray is first to reach for a glass. The rest follow and soon, chatter is brimming up as Bonny, on the periphery, watches the guests perform as at a cocktail party. She looks perplexed and suddenly announces, in a rather petulant tone, "A wedding is a serious business."

"Should a wedding be 'a serious business'?" the lawyer asks her. "I would think the day should be quite ebullient."

"Of course," she says, changing her tone. "It is such a happy occasion – any wedding – and of course, when it is one's own…" and she smiles a brilliant smile.

Brit turns away and mumbles to me, "This is almost too hard to watch," and I agree, saying, "I wish I didn't dislike her so, but it's hard to forgive…what she did."

"I know, darling, I know," he says. "Life is often unfair and this woman has been beyond venal. Still…"

As the party gains momentum, Sasha snapping away at one and all, Franco raises a glass of *Le Couvent Cabernet Sauvignon*. "I toast a day to remember in the brand new wine from this *château*, the first pressing. May you all enjoy it!" he exclaims, proudly. For some reason – maybe nerves – we all clap.

Suddenly, there is a distant sound. At first it seems to be the braying of an animal – a donkey or a mule. But then, one realizes, as the sound grows closer and louder, it is the hee-haw siren of a French police car.

Franco leaves the salon and goes through the entry hall to the front door, which he flings open as René Poignal dismounts the vehicle in the driveway, crosses the gravel and enters the *château*.

"The best man has arrived," Franco announces to the guests who have been drawn into the entry hall by the sound of the siren and the crunching of gravel. Bonny stands at the front of the little group, her eyes wide with anticipation.

"Giscard?" she says, beginning to glance wildly about.

"I am sorry Madame," René says formally. "But my brother has been called away – back to Barcelona. Unexpected circumstances in his business forced him to leave Paris abruptly…"

"What?" Bonny shrieks. "He is gone? You were supposed to bring him?" and she rushes towards the policeman.

"Now, now, Madame," René is saying as he fends off her small raised fists. "*Calmez-vous, s'il vous plaît. Calmez, Madame.*" René manages to catch both her hands in one of his own, reaches into his back pocket for a pair of handcuffs, and clips them around the wrists of the distraught Bonny.

"What are you doing?" she screams. By now, tears are flowing down her cheeks in angry black rivulets. "Take your hands off me – and these..." she says, shaking the cuffs behind her back. "Remove these," she says shrilly.

"I am sorry Madame Brandeis, but I am actually here to arrest you for attempted identity theft, stolen private information in terms of credit cards, and attempted fraud in regard to the purchase of a house."

"That was Hamad al-Boudi," she is shrieking. "It was all his idea about the house... and it's that damn woman, Elizabeth..." Turning to me, she shouts, "This is all your fault. You set me up...You've always been out to get me...I hate you, Elizabeth.... So does Hamad al-Boudi...He brought me to Paris... to...to..." Bonny is sputtering.

"Madame Brandeis," Jacques Ballon interjects. " It is you who went to the Chase Bank in New York impersonating Madame Elizabeth, granted at Hamad al-Boudi's instigation, but it was you who perpetrated the fraud." Then to René, he says, "You will see all this in a copy of the brief for the law suit I will send you." René nods to the lawyer, as he clutches Bonny's arm. She is wriggling.

Sasha has been snapping pictures rapidly throughout this whole encounter.

"And Giscard? He would not leave of his own volition. You must have sent him away," Bonny says, turning to me, her face contorted, vicious.

"Now, how could I possibly do that?" I ask.

"Indeed she did no such thing," René says in a formidable voice. "Madame, I know my brother. You have to understand Giscard."

"I do. I do," Bonny shouts. "And he understands me. He loves me. He is mad for me."

"No, no, Madame, you're wrong. Giscard is only mad for love."

With that, René Poignal, fulfilling his policeman's duty with a hand beneath her arm, takes Bonny Brandeis through the entry foyer and out into a now cold, rainy evening, her blonde head bowed as he places her into the police car.

We all stand and watch this scene with varying degrees of angst and pity, but also with a sense of justice. There is silence as we stand there, shifting from one foot to another. Sue, always resilient, suddenly exclaims, "Thank God that's over. Come in, come in, everyone," and she leads the way back into the salon where Willie Blakely greets us with a tray of *paté de foie gras hors d'oeuvres* and a bubbling cheese *fondue* on the bar table with pieces of *baguette* surrounding it for us to dip.

As we walk into the grand salon, I hear Ray ask Sasha, "You get some good ones?" indicating the camera Sasha is holding.

"You could say so. After all, I've worked in many a war zone," Sasha replies with a wry grin. "This was comparable."

I turn to Brit. "I guess I'm glad," I say softly. "But the ending to Bonny Brandeis...it was pretty pitiful."

"I know what you mean, darling," is his reply. Then, with a sigh, he adds, "Giscard may be mad for love, but I am mad for you," and he leans to me with a kiss.

Which I return.

CHAPTER 25

Finale

IT'S MONDAY AND reality is setting in. After a loving night with Brit and the usual *café/croissant* breakfast, this morning, shared in my room on the 5th floor, it is time to make a plan. Thanksgiving is only a bit over a month away, and I am remiss in returning to my New York obligations.

"I am going to have to leave Paris, once again," I say sadly. "How I hate to go because it means I have to leave you too," and tears fill my eyes.

"I know," he says. "I miss you already," and he hugs me tight.

I disentangle myself slowly, from the sweet embrace, and reach for the phone, booking a ticket on American Airlines for the following Wednesday from Charles de Gaulle to Kennedy in New York. It's the usual morning flight that arrives mid afternoon, on what they now call a 'comfort coach' reservation. *Tant pis.*

We have arranged to lunch with Sue and Franco at *Caviar Kaspia* at 1:00 o'clock. The last moments at the *château's* fantasy 'wedding' had been, not exactly dark, but somewhat somber. Although no one had real sympathy for Bonny Brandeis, the vision of her being carted off, half-hysterical, in handcuffs, is not a picture anyone wants to remember.

On the banquette at the lovely Russian restaurant, with its soft balalaika music and obsequious waiter who places the requisite vodka in its small silver bucket on the table, Brit and I sit side by side. Rarely have I felt this close to someone. The communion between us needs no words, and we bask in the sense of wellness between us.

In short order, our two friends appear, Sue, especially lovely in a camel hair, fitted coat, and Franco, his dark looks made ruddy by the iciness of the street. They bring a wave of refreshing coldness from the outside weather, as they plunk down beside us, that awakens and animates.

"I'm for the smoked salmon. It is superb here – served with hot toast, a bit of melted butter and pepper, the best anywhere," Franco announces with enthusiasm. "I don't have to see a menu."

"Sounds delicious," Brit pipes in. "I'll have that too."

"For me, the usual," Sue says equally enthusiastic. "Baked potato, fluffed up with sour cream, and beluga on top."

"Me too," I say, in a sufficiently moderate voice, to have the three turn to me and ask, in unison, "what's the matter?"

I look at them, Sue, Franco, my Brit. I have already mentally placed myself on the airplane leaving France and am sad. "It's just that the time has come for me to go, to return to the States. So much of my person is left in this country – with you, both of you, and Brit and Jean-Luc, Isabella…it's as if I leave my soul behind." My voice is choked.

"Ah, darling," Sue says, touching my hand. "Paris isn't going anywhere. We," and she turns to Franco who is gazing at her, "we aren't going anywhere. Surely Brit is yours for the taking and the Marcel pair? They adore you."

Her words touch me, and it is just as well that the enticing plates arrive to distract us and me, in particular, from an over-emotional moment.

As Franco prepares his toast, the melted butter over the pink salmon, as he cracks the pepper mill high over the dish and sprays the tiny black specks over his masterpiece, he says, "I wonder what Bonny is having for her midday meal?" and we all burst into laughter.

"Ah, poor woman," says Sue. "I wonder what's to become of her."

"I doubt she'll do much jail time," Franco continues. "Hamad al-Boudi is pretty powerful..."

"You mean, he's pretty rich," Brit interjects.

"He'll probably spring her somehow – bribes to the Paris police," Franco adds.

"Not René Poignal!" I say emphatically. "He is much too proper... much too by the book."

"No, not René. I agree," says Brit, "but Bonny is probably in the hands of other city officials. They are very...'approachable?' – if that's the word," Brit adds somewhat cynically.

We linger over espresso and *amaretto* well into the afternoon, four friends saying a lingering goodbye. Sue and Franco have their car parked on the side street. We leave them with hugs and touches, in front of the glass encased storefront of *Caviar Kaspia*, through which one enters to go upstairs to the elegant restaurant.

Brit and I find a taxi at a nearby taxi stand, which swoops us past La Madeleine and heads to the Marais district and Brit's small house that has become a haven for the two of us. We spend our final night and the next day together, as lovers do, and on Tuesday, late in the day after an *omelette/champagne* brunch, I return alone to the Hotel Marcel to pack mournfully and prepare for the flight next day. Mounir, the Moroccan driver, is booked to take me to the airport at 10:00 AM. Jean-Luc and Isabella will join me for breakfast in the salon for a final *aurevoir*.

Brit had wanted to take me to the plane, but I refused, telling him how cruel a public parting can feel to me. We have said it all to each other. We have planned for a reunion in early spring. We are drained of further emotion.

So I *partir*, solo.

Once in my seat on the aircraft, I dream of every moment of my sojourn, tracing the steps that I have taken, envisioning the faces I have seen, in my time.

Home seems mundane, but the bustle and activity pick me up and I hurl forward into the old life, leaving the dream of Paris days enclosed in my heart – even the ridiculous saga of Bonny Brandeis.

I learn from Sue, later, shortly before Christmas, in fact, that Bonny Brandeis had indeed been sprung from the French jail through Hamad al-Boudi's machinations and bribery. She is now living in Doha, the capital of Qatar – forced to wear a burka and do the bidding of Hamad – (substitute an 'e' for the 'i' in bidding). She buys a lot of Victoria's Secret lingerie on line.

She is, apparently, kept in a grand little apartment overlooking the water in a nearby cove, where she can dress as she likes, but on the street, she must be covered. She does not dare go out burka-less, because Hamad's men are in constant watch over her residence and movements. Hamad has no intention of ever letting what happened to his daughter Lilith – her running free in stylish dress in Paris – occur here in Qatar, to his newest acquisition – Bonny Brandeis. Sue is sure that Bonny is fully aware that the Arab sheikh would do her ill, should she break his trust.

"I'll just bet she's scared to death," was Sue's comment to me in her long letter. "I'm also sure Bonny is awaiting anxiously the old sheikh's loss of interest in her – when he will require a newer, younger version of herself. At least, then she will be free. As of now, she is nothing but his prisoner."

I clutch this letter to me. Poor Bonny Brandeis, and then, on rereading Sue's narrative again, I find the fate of Bonny Brandeis, deeply satisfying.

EPILOGUE

Paris

WHATEVER LOVE, ADMIRATION, expectation you bring to Paris, comes back to you in full. Like a reverberating reflection, the City of Light mirrors back the gift you bring, enhanced. It adds its own special aura and endows your present with an everlasting glow, and there is never any *finis*.

For each one of us, the experience, the emotion, is different. To me, I cherish my time wrapped in the arms of the city, enthralled on its streets, encased in a wondrous world of kings and queens and massive steeds; of bells and churches and children at the puppet show in the *parc*; of chestnut trees and *fleurs de lis* and *fraises des bois*; the scent of *café* and *chocolat* and *cognac* in the air; and lovely *demoiselles* in stylish clothes who pass me by.

And then, there is the Hotel Marcel, with its charming hotelier/owner, an elevator like a coffin, a balcony above the avenue, and the windows in the apartments across the street through which one can see into Paris domesticity of the most dramatic kind. How irresistible!

I grow fascinated with secret schemes, of entanglements and intricate affairs, some clandestine, some mystifying, and always the riddle, the enigma that each personality evokes.

And then there is Brit, like none other in my life. He presents no enigma at all. He gives me so much to anticipate, springtime, together again, sharing days of art, food, friends, exploring Paris, the city of dreams.

Now that's a promise to believe in. And I do.

AUTHORS NOTE

THE LIGHT THAT IS PARIS WILL NEVER BE DIMMED

There is no way that the spirit of France, the resilience of its citizens, the courage of Parisians, will be cowed by the cowardly and vicious attacks of the past months.

Since Caesar's Rome invaded, since the Huns crossed into France, since British kings forded the English Channel, since the Vikings rowed ships down the Seine, since World War I and the blood spilled in Brittany, since Hitler's occupation of Paris in World War II, the bravery, the stoicism, the faith of the French has prevailed.

Paris, its capital, has been there for it all. The city is not going anywhere, and the joyous life it inspires will surely resurge.

The bistros' casualness. The stadium's thrill. The sound of music.

And the delight and welcome of a small hotel.

Elizabeth Cooke

CPSIA information can be obtained at www.ICGtesting.com
Printed in the USA
LVOW07s0333090216

474255LV00001BB/68/P